"I Know You'll Love This," She Said, Yanking Off the Cover.

I looked down at the squiggly black things that I'd seen earlier in the refrigerator. "What are they?"

"Tarantula legs," she said calmly. "A special treat."

"No kidding." This was getting interesting. Kids usually do crazy things to test their babysitters. I knew that. I was prepared. I even enjoyed seeing what they would think up.

Still, with all my vast experience with kids, nobody had ever offered me tarantula legs for dessert before. These kids were really funny and I wanted to make a good impression. So I laughed and put one of the "legs" in my mouth. . . .

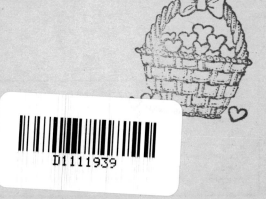

SAMANTHA SLADE: MONSTER-SITTER

SUSAN SMITH

Produced by
The Philip Lief Group, Inc.

AN ARCHWAY PAPERBACK
Published by POCKET BOOKS
New York   London   Toronto   Sydney   Tokyo

AN ARCHWAY PAPERBACK *Original*

An Archway Paperback published by
POCKET BOOKS, a division of Simon & Schuster Inc.
1230 Avenue of the Americas, New York, NY 10020

ISBN: 0-671-63713-4

First Archway Paperback printing October 1987

10 9 8 7 6 5 4 3 2

To Philip Lief,
Kevin Osborn and Pat MacDonald

SAMANTHA SLADE:
MONSTER-SITTER

Chapter

1

Wanted: Babysitter for three lovable monsters. Two to three days/evenings per week, sometimes on weekends. Good pay. Please call 200-2000.

It was three weeks before Halloween when I noticed this ad in the paper. I had been looking for a new job—bigger opportunities—for a while. My paper route just wasn't doing it for me.

So I circled the ad with a felt pen and called the number. I had one of those weird feelings that I get sometimes, like I know something's going to happen. I'm not saying that I can see into the future because whenever I try that, I just come up with this gray area. But I knew my life was going to change. I knew it the moment I spoke to Dr. Anastasia Brown.

"The Halloween season is the perfect time

to meet new people," she said to me over the telephone, which you must admit, was a pretty funny thing to say.

Just as I hung up the phone, my friend Iris came over. Of course, I told Iris about the job and that I was going to see Dr. Brown.

Iris was dressed as a slice of Swiss cheese, her freckled face peering through one of the holes in her cardboard costume. She wanted to show me what she was wearing for Halloween. After weeks of thought, she had finally come up with the perfect look.

"Who's Dr. Brown?" she asked. "I've never heard of her."

"I think the Browns are new in town. Don't worry, I'll let you know all the details," I said. "Hey, would you watch Patrick for me? I won't be long."

"Sure," she said. "Good luck."

"Thanks," I told her, as I yanked on my blue jean jacket. "I'll see you later."

I hopped on my bicycle, leaving Iris at my house with a brand-new bag of potato chips and my bratty little brother Patrick. I thought about Halloween costumes. For the second year in a row, I planned to wear my cat suit: a black leotard with a tail, pipe cleaner whiskers, and ears pinned onto a headband. With my short black hair and green eyes I look pretty authentic. It's not very original, but I leave originality to Iris at Halloween.

By the way, my name is Samantha, and I'm twelve. Samantha Slade—big sister, ping-pong player, and babysitter extraordinaire. The extraordinaire part comes later. And I'm so glad I got to use that word.

The Browns lived at 101 Morris Avenue, in the suburban town where I live, Plainview, New Jersey. The house looked like every other house on the block—brown with white shutters, a white picket fence, a couple of fruit trees out front. But the lawn hadn't been mowed, the flowers looked a little dry, and the house looked kind of unlived in. I made a mental note to ask Iris whether she knew who had lived there before the Browns.

I opened the gate. "Hello? Anyone there?" I cried.

"Hallooo!" A tall woman dressed in black popped her head out from behind a spiky berry bush. She had tied little tinkling bells on the ends of her long black hair. "Oh, there you are! You must be Samantha. Such a lovely name—we once had a rattlesnake named Samantha."

"That's an interesting pet," I said, trying to make conversation.

"I'm Dr. Brown." She extended her hand, revealing sharply pointed fingernails.

"Nice to meet you," I said politely.

"I'll find the children so that you can meet them. I must warn you, they are awfully spirited." Dr. Brown sighed as she led the way up the path, which was bordered by untended flower beds. "They get into lots of mischief, my two little horrors."

"Oh, that's okay, Dr. Brown. I'm used to monsters. My brother Patrick is really awful," I said confidently. "If I can take care of Patrick, I can take care of anyone."

"That's so nice to know," she said. As we rounded the corner of the house, Dr. Brown waved to a young girl of about ten. "Here's Lupi. Meet Samantha, Lupi."

I said hello to a pretty girl whose shaggy blond hair hung over her huge blue eyes. She looked like she should be an actress on television, and I told her so.

Lupi smiled.

"I haven't seen you around," I said.

"That's because we just moved here," Lupi replied.

"How do you like school?" I asked.

"I don't go to school. Drake and I have a tutor."

"Our tutor is lovely, really," Dr. Brown said, sighing her little sigh as she led the way into the house. Then she padded down a long narrow hallway, motioning for me to follow. She entered a room which looked like one of those science laboratories in an old Boris Karloff movie. Hisses and bubbling sounds filled the whole room. A dark-haired boy of about eight was bending over a flask of smoking white stuff.

"Wow, this is some chemistry set!" I exclaimed.

"Yes it is," Dr. Brown agreed. "I am a scientist, and my son enjoys the laboratory. Meet my son Drake." She kissed the top of the boy's slick black hair affectionately.

He grinned at me. "Pleased to meet you." He spoke with a funny accent—just what you'd expect.

I giggled. "Great accent, Drake. You sound like a real mad scientist."

Drake smiled.

"The children are very different, as you can see," Dr. Brown said as we left the laboratory. "There's also my sister's baby, Kimmie, who's asleep at the moment. She's with us some of the time, a real little mover. Lupi gets a little hairy at times, and Drake is a darling, but he has rather exotic tastes."

"Oh, what *do* the kids eat, by the way? Anything special?" I asked eagerly. My own parents are really strict about sugar, so I love to babysit at houses where chocolate cake is a regular in the fridge.

"Oh, yes, very special—but I'll let them acquaint you with their favorites," said Dr. Brown.

We went into the living room. It was decorated with a few odd things for Halloween. For instance, instead of curtains in the living room, a big spiderweb covered the window. A bearskin with the head still on it hung on the wall over the fireplace. A big cauldron sat in the hearth—I had seen one of them once before on a school field trip to one of those reconstructed colonial villages. Everything else looked pretty normal, and I guess that's why these things stood out.

"We just moved in here and we haven't decorated the house quite to our liking," said Dr. Brown. "The people before us had rather strange tastes. It is rather a plain house, don't you think?"

"It's a nice house," I said, just to keep the conversation going. To be honest, I had never given much thought to houses before.

"We do have our own style, though," she said, smiling. "I'm hoping my husband will bring us some lovely things from one of his voyages. Sit down, Samantha."

I sat down on a big couch covered with animal skins. I was wondering if someone in the family was a taxidermist when a loud squeak erupted from the cushion under me. I gasped.

"Oh, it's nothing. Just Scream, one of the children's toys," Dr. Brown explained. "There it is."

I looked down at the cushion. The "toy" was a squishy rubber face with a scrunched-up mouth. When I pressed the toy, its mouth opened and it screamed. I sat with Scream in my lap while Dr. Brown explained the job.

"I will pay you six dollars an hour for babysitting," she said.

"You're kidding!" I exclaimed. I know that's not the sort of thing you're supposed to say on interviews, but I couldn't help it.

"Is that not enough?" Dr. Brown blinked her black eyes at me.

"Oh, no. It's fine," I said quickly. It was twice as much money as I had expected! Nobody I knew made that much babysitting, or doing anything else either! "I'll do it. I'd love to babysit for you. The kids seem like fun, and I'm sure we'll get along."

"Yes, I sense that you will," said Dr. Brown. I suddenly noticed that she was sitting in a chair with holes all through it. I wondered if the old tenants of the house had left it behind.

Dr. Brown rose. "Well, it was lovely meeting you, Samantha." She made the "s" stand out in my name—as if she were hissing—sort of like a snake. "And I look forward to seeing you again, Friday night at seven."

"Great. Thanks a lot." I shook her hand again, carefully avoiding her pointy finger-nails. I was surprised that Dr. Brown hadn't asked me for any references. "I guess my mother will want to talk to you," I said.

"Oh, yes, of course, dear," said Dr. Brown.

As I walked down the hallway, I noticed that all the houseplants were dead. Houseplants are easy to forget about. I'm always getting yelled at when I forget to water them at home. And Scruples, our cat, gets in trouble for digging up their soil.

Right then, I felt so grown up. I've always had a job of some kind. And I always have money, so Patrick and Iris know they can borrow from me.

But this was the greatest job I'd ever had—interesting, high-paying, challenging—all the things they say in those career advertisements on TV. I hopskipped down the path, dodging a sticker bush. I couldn't wait to tell Iris.

Chapter

===2===

"I got the job!" I announced when I found Iris standing in the kitchen, making milkshakes.

She turned around. A smear of chocolate ran across her cheek. "Congratulations," she said, grinning.

"Guess what I'm getting paid?"

"Oh, let's see—fifty thousand dollars a year?" She poured me a milkshake.

"Almost," I told her. "Six dollars an hour!"

"Yeah, you're right, I *was* close," Iris said. "How's the shake?"

"Good. Fabulous." We went out onto the patio to sit down. "Hey, Iris. Who lived in the Browns' house before them?"

"The Soul family—your basic, ordinary people," said Iris. "So are the kids really monsters?"

"Well, I don't know yet. I just met them.

Their mother says they are, but you know how mothers are."

"Mothers always say that. But remember, a babysitter is fair game," warned Iris. "They're like substitute teachers."

"Hey, I never thought of it that way," I said. "Except everybody gets used to their babysitter eventually. You never get used to a sub because that's all she is—a sub."

"Maybe you're getting danger pay," suggested Iris blackly. "Did I ever tell you about my uncle who painted the Golden Gate Bridge orange? Know what happened to him?"

Iris was always telling me stories about her relatives in order to prove some point. "No, what?"

Iris drew her finger across her throat. "He died."

"Well, I'm sorry to hear that, but I don't see what any of this has to do with me. A lot of people die, Iris. That's nothing new." I sighed. Iris Martin is my best friend, but sometimes she can be a pain.

"Just thought you'd be interested," she mumbled, her voice echoing into her empty glass. Suddenly she said, "Hey, what about the Halloween committee? We've got to come up with something."

I'd been so busy thinking about getting a job that I forgot I was head of the Halloween party at school. Actually, so far, Iris and I *were* the committee. Nobody else had volunteered, so our homeroom teacher, Ms. Snell, had appointed us.

"Well, you first, Samantha," urged my friend.

Iris always expects me to come up with the ideas for these kinds of things. She just sits around until I come up with something good, and then she really starts rolling with her own ideas. We make a pretty good team that way. But sometimes in the beginning I get irritated because I know I'm supposed to start the thinking.

"Well, first, let's figure out what kind of party it's going to be," I said.

"Last year all the teachers dressed up and tried to scare the kids, remember?"

"Oh, yeah, that's right." My mind stopped on the word "scare." My mind works like that—it just goes along until I hear or see something and get jolted, and I just have to stop right there. In this case, the word "scare" zonked me.

"I've got it," I announced to Iris.

"What?"

"An idea. Let's do a haunted house."

Her eyes widened. "Hey, that's a great idea! Now why didn't I think of that?"

(That's Iris' standard response, by the way.)

She jumped up and started pacing up and down the room. No one ever saw a slice of

Swiss cheese move quite that fast. "That's terrific. We could have all kinds of scary things like blood and bugs and snakes."

Once she got started like this, there was no stopping Iris. "I can borrow some of Patrick's masks. He has some horrible ones," I said.

Then she looked at me. "Where's it going to be?" she asked.

She always gives me the major technical problems and she gets to think up all the fun stuff. "We'll cross that bridge when we come to it. I think we're doing pretty well. Hey, all this thinking is making me hungry. Where are those potato chips?"

"Patrick has them."

I followed a trail of potato-chip crumbs into the den, where Patrick had his eyes glued to the TV set. Some horrible cartoon was blasting away—one of those things our parents don't approve of, but I let him watch them just to keep him out of my hair.

"Chips, please," I said.

Without moving his gaze from the screen, he handed me the empty bag. I stared inside it. "Gee, thanks, Pig," I said. "Do you realize this bag of chips cost a dollar, twenty-nine?"

"Big deal."

That was Patrick's favorite phrase. "This bag of chips was meant to feed all three of us," I went on.

He didn't answer. "I just got a great babysitting job," I said.

He finally spoke. "Poor kids."

I poured the rest of the potato-chip crumbs over his head.

As I had expected, my mother decided she had to meet the Browns before I could babysit for them, so she went to their house right after she got home.

When she returned, she said, "Nice people, except they're a little strange. Their house is a bit messy, but I realize they haven't really settled in yet. I love the Halloween decorations in their living room. Really creative," she went on.

I went to the Browns' to babysit on Friday night. My mother dropped me off on her way to pick up Patrick from a friend's house. She was in a big hurry as usual and hadn't had time to put her shoes on, so she said, "Say hi for me, will you, honey?"

"Okay," I said, relieved. My mother always embarrasses me. She doesn't look that bad—in fact, my friends think she's good-looking—but I never know what she's going to say. She has black hair like mine and the same green eyes, and she's always in a hurry or in some way not together. She always seems really absent-minded and preoccupied. She's really a great mother, but she needs constant reminders. Sometimes I think she should pin notes to her shirt so she can remember everything.

I slid out of the car and waited for her to drive down the block before I rang the doorbell. A tall, dark-haired man answered the door.

"Let me introduce myself," he said in a monotone. "I am Frank Brown." He extended his hand to me. I noticed that his suit was very old-fashioned and looked limp, as though it had come from a vintage clothing shop.

Dr. Brown slithered up beside him and wove her arm affectionately through his.

They made a bizarre couple. She wore this droopy black dress with lots of folds and a tattered hem. I thought maybe she was into the punk look.

"Nice to meet you," I said politely.

"We loved meeting your mother," said Mr. Brown.

"Cousin Kimmie is staying with us this evening," Dr. Brown explained. "You don't mind watching her, too, do you?"

"Oh, not at all," I replied.

Lupi came into the hall wearing a werewolf costume. I hardly recognized her as she took my hand in her furry one. "My brother is making dinner. Come with me and I'll show you," she urged. I'd never seen such a convincing costume: her eyes even looked yellow.

I noticed a shrunken head hanging from the mantelpiece.

"Nice decorations," I commented. Boy, I thought to myself, these Browns really take Halloween seriously.

After the Browns had left for their party, Lupi led me through the house to the kitchen.

"Hello, Samantha," said Drake, as he stirred something on the stove that looked like hamburger. "I'm cooking blood pudding. Have you ever had it?"

"Uh, no." It sounded gross, but I didn't want to say so.

"It's a Mexican dish—fried blood really— and it's so delicious." An impish expression spread over his face.

"I can't wait," I said, gulping. "Is this the Halloween special?"

"Oh, and wait until you see what's for dessert!" exclaimed Lupi.

I shuddered to think. Suddenly I heard a wild shrieking outside. It sounded like a cat fight.

Lupi peered out the kitchen window. "Oh, there's my cousin, Kimmie," she said calmly. We went outside to find her.

The backyard was even more overgrown than the front. I tramped behind Lupi, following her exact steps.

"How old is your cousin?" I asked, remembering that Dr. Brown had said she was a baby.

"That's not an easy question to answer," Lupi responded, then changed the subject. "We have a swimming pool back here."

Sure enough, we came to a huge murky pool with water so green, you couldn't even see to the bottom. A black cat, yowling his head off, swam across it.

"What's the cat doing in the pool?" I shouted.

A thin little girl of about three stood next to the pool. She had long, red hair and more freckles than anyone I've ever seen. She pointed at the cat. "I wanted to see if he could swim," she said in a loud, clear voice. "And he can!"

"That's Kimmie," explained Lupi. "She's always doing things like this."

I leaned over the pool and grabbed the terrified cat, who dug his claws into my chest. "Ouch!"

"We'll put him in the oven to dry him out," I said teasingly. My arms and the poor cat were covered with green slime from the water.

"He would taste good," Lupi said.

I laughed nervously. Lupi sure had a strange sense of humor. "Roast cat and fried blood. What a disgusting combination."

We brought Kimmie and the cat inside. In the kitchen, I rubbed the cat dry with a towel and put him by the fire. "What's the cat's name?" I asked.

"Claws," answered Drake. "Dinner's ready."

I put out the silverware and Lupi got out plates. We set the table for four and sat Kimmie down on the top of a telephone book so she could reach the table. She moved the silverware around until it finally suited her, but it looked totally messed up to me.

Drake had burned the tortillas until they were all black. I could understand why someone might want to miss dinner.

"Shouldn't we heat up some more tortillas?" I suggested.

Drake stared at me, straight-faced. "No. We like them this way," he said, placing the tortillas on the table.

After we all sat down, I spooned some of the "fried blood" onto each of the plates. At first Kimmie just pushed hers around with a spoon, but she finally managed a mouthful.

I went into the kitchen for a glass of water. Somehow I had lost my appetite. The "blood" looked like hamburger, but it sure didn't look very tasty next to those black tortillas. I peeked in the refrigerator to see if there was anything else to eat, but nothing appealed to me. There was a dish of something the color of uncooked shrimp, some black squiggly things, and some lemonade.

"This is good!" I heard Kimmie cry, but when I came back, she and her plate had disappeared. I was just about to ask what had happened to her when a funny giggle rose from under the table, and then—splat!—a black tortilla landed on my plate. Drake threw his tortilla at Lupi, hitting her in the face. They all started to laugh.

I opened my mouth to play the serious babysitter. "Now come on, kids, let's not throw the food around." But I know how much Iris and I like to have whipped-cream fights. So it was hard to act serious when everyone, including me, was having such a good time. And I figured we could all clean up the mess later.

Well, anyway, next they started to throw the blood pudding. It was really getting a little out of hand. I tasted the blood pudding, and decided that it was pretty good. Wow! Surprise, surprise.

When everyone had emptied their plates, Kimmie clambered up from under the table, and Lupi got up to take the dessert out of the refrigerator.

"I know you'll love this," she said, yanking off the cover.

I looked down at the squiggly black things

that I'd seen earlier in the refrigerator. "What are they?"

"Tarantula legs," she said calmly. "A special treat."

"No kidding." This was getting interesting. Kids usually do crazy things to test their babysitters. I knew that. I was prepared. I even enjoyed seeing what they would think up.

Still, with all my vast experience with kids, nobody had ever offered me tarantula legs for dessert before. These kids were really funny and I wanted to make a good impression. So I just laughed and put one of the "legs" in my mouth.

Chapter

3

On Saturday, Iris came over to my house. When I told her about the tarantula legs, she laughed.

"What did they taste like?" she wanted to know.

"They were okay, a little dry and chewy," I told her. "I think they were really Chinese fried noodles."

"Probably. But what a great gag to pull on a sitter," Iris said. "Wish I'd been there. Maybe we can use Chinese fried noodles for the haunted house."

We were making a list of stuff we could do for the haunted house before going to the mall to buy a few things.

"What about the skeleton from the science room?" suggested Iris.

"Great," I said. "We can put a blinking light on him."

"Samantha, would you check the pasta, please?" my mother called from another part of the house. "Hurry up—I think it might be boiling over."

I yelled yes, and skipped through the hallway. As I turned the corner, I ran smack into the vacuum cleaner, then fell on top of it, which made it start up. I screamed.

"Sam?" my mother called. Iris came down the hall. Patrick emerged from his room and stood laughing at me.

"Don't just stand there. Get this stupid thing out of the hall," I yelled at him, but he was useless. He had doubled over with laughter.

Iris proved to be useless, also. A big grin spread across her face. "I've got an idea, Sam."

"Right now?" I muttered, turning off the vacuum and examining my bruised knee.

"Let's take a vacuum cleaner and put a sheet over it. Then turn it on—varoom!" she sang in delight. "It can be a ghost—get it?"

I scowled at her. "Uh-huh, really great. When do you ever stop?"

"Sam! The pasta!" my mother cried out. I ran into the kitchen and pulled the pasta pot off the stove. Then I threw a strand of the spaghetti at the wall to see if it stuck. That was our old family recipe for seeing if spaghetti was ready. Of course, we only did it with spaghetti and linguine, never with shells or elbow macaroni. When the strand stuck, I drained the spaghetti and put it back in the pot to cool. My mother was planning on making a cold pasta salad which she's famous for.

"I've got another idea," said Iris. "How about using spaghetti as worms? The lights are out . . ."

"And the spaghetti is cold and slippery," I added.

We both laughed. I added "spaghetti" to our list, which already included these items:

1. Slime with Eyeballs
2. Creepy Crawlies
3. Vacuum cleaner
4. White sheet

We rode our bikes to the mall to look for some of the things on our list. We thought we'd find most of them at this magic shop called The Crystal Ball—it was supposed to have nearly anything you'd ever need to scare somebody half to death. Usually the store didn't get much business, but of course it was packed with people because Halloween was coming up and the store also rented Halloween costumes.

In the window we saw a gorilla and a silver-foil space creature costume with a grotesque head. There seemed to be a rush on space creature costumes and a couple of customers stood at the counter, fighting over a tinfoil suit.

"Hey, look at this," said Iris. Inside one of the glass cases, a lifelike hand moved. It almost looked as if it were beckoning us toward it.

"We *have* to have one of those," Iris told me. "How much is it?"

I asked the salesclerk.

"Ten dollars, dear," the clerk said, frowning as though she couldn't understand why anyone would buy such a thing.

"Okay, we'll take it." I didn't even consult with Iris, because I figured we needed this.

"Here's the Slime," I said, pointing to the little green tubs on the counter, next to the cash register. Iris and I checked our money. We only had twenty dollars to spend, and we still wanted to get some other things.

"I haven't got all day, girls," the clerk grumbled.

"We really need Slime," Iris said. "What's a haunted house without Slime?"

It all sounded so logical that we decided to buy everything. Then we went into Woolworth's and found some Creepy Crawlies, which are little creatures slimy to the touch. Iris found a big string spiderweb, so we bought that, too.

"We can always use our allowances if we see something else we have to have. Ms. Snell will pay us back," Iris said.

"What about the budget?" I asked, because I'm always concerned about money, no matter whose it is.

"Nobody's going to care about the budget once they hear about our wonderful idea," Iris insisted.

"You're probably right."

A few blocks from home, we went into the corner store where Tommy Deere works. I've had sort of a crush on Tommy Deere for about a year. His father owns the store and I try not to go there too often, because I'm always self-conscious and afraid he might find out I like him.

When we walked in, Tommy was working at the meat counter, so he didn't see us. His face was half hidden behind the meat tenderizer and packaged sauces. After Iris and I chose an ice-cream bar each, Mr. Deere called Tommy to come up front.

Carefully I got out my change to pay for the ice cream.

"Hi, Samantha. Hi, Iris," Tommy said. He had dark brown hair and a little scar next to his mouth. He was wearing a green T-shirt that said "Smile Sourpuss" on the front.

"Hi, Tommy," we chorused, and then we had to laugh because it sounded so funny.

"Hey, Tommy, want to join our Halloween committee?" Iris asked.

Furiously, I jabbed her with my elbow. I felt my face getting hot.

"Huh?" He blinked at her in confusion.

"We're the members of the Halloween party committee," I said, making it sound like we were a couple of Girl Scouts, "and we just bought all sorts of stuff for the party—you know, things like Slime."

"Oh, yeah, great," he mumbled. "I've seen that stuff. It's pretty gross."

"Want to join?" Iris asked again. "We need extra help."

I could've killed her. Honestly, how could she do this to me? My face must've been absolutely purple by that time.

Someone had to put a stop to her. I stamped on her toe.

"Ouch!" she cried out.

Tommy grinned and blushed. "Naw, I can't, sorry," he said. "I've got basketball practice after school almost every day."

"That's okay," I said quickly, relieved that he had said no. What would we have done if he had said yes?

Hugging my package containing the battery-operated hand and the Slime, I bolted for the open door.

"Hey, Samantha!" Tommy yelled. "Don't you want your ice cream?"

I whirled around. Sure enough, I'd left the double-crunch bar on the counter. "Oh, uh, thanks," I mumbled. "Well, see you later."

"See you," Tommy said.

Outside the store, Iris whooped with laughter.

"It's not that funny," I said in a huff. "How'd you like it if I did that to you? I could've killed you!"

Iris said, "I thought it'd be fun to have him around."

"What if he had said yes? I wouldn't be able to think of a thing for the party with him around," I said miserably.

"Why not?" she demanded. "He's a nice guy."

Iris was being much too sensible for my liking—especially right after she had acted so dumb. So I said, "Maybe, but I don't want him around when I've got to do some serious thinking." Actually, I'm sure I could think just fine around anybody else *but* him.

Iris scoffed. "You're crazy, Sam! You must be going through a phase."

"Must be."

When we got back to my house, we laid all

our purchases out on the rug. I couldn't believe how much everything had cost, but Iris reminded me that I was always complaining about the cost of things.

Iris set up the battery-operated hand and we put my cat, Scruples, in front of it. Scruples stiffened, her hair standing on end, and then she hissed and ran off. We laughed.

Later that evening, I put the hand in Patrick's bed and turned down the light. By eight-thirty, his usual bedtime, I had nearly forgotten about the hand. Suddenly a bloodcurdling scream sprang from the bedroom.

My mother and father nearly jumped out of their seats. "Patrick?" Mom hurried in the direction of his room.

My father peered at me over the rim of his glasses. "Samantha, what's the matter with your brother?" he asked, as though he had guessed I had something to do with it.

"I don't know," I said innocently enough.

Just then we heard my mother scream. When Dad shot me a puzzled glance, I knew my minutes were numbered.

With Patrick clinging to her for dear life, my mother marched back into the living room. She looked ready to explode—not a pretty sight.

"Samantha, get that *thing* out of your brother's room right this instant!" she cried.

"But, Mom, it was just a joke," I tried to explain. "We got this stuff at . . ."

She cut me off abruptly. "I don't care where you got it. Get it out of there NOW!"

I ran in to get my hand, which was still moving in spite of everything. I picked it up and turned it off.

My parents followed me into the bedroom as though they didn't believe I could have done such a thing, but my father laughed when he saw the hand. At least one family member could see the humor in all this.

"Why in the world did you get that horrible thing?" my mother wanted to know.

"For our Halloween party at school," I told her. "I'm the head of the committee. I'm supposed to buy things like this and Slime and Creepy Crawlies."

Dad rolled his eyes, exchanging glances with my mother.

"Okay, but no more practical jokes with this stuff, Samantha," Dad said.

"Or you're grounded," added my mother. "That's the most frightening thing I've ever seen."

"Me, too," said Patrick, still clinging to his mommy like a scared baby. I glared at him.

After they saw the hand safely stuffed into a paper bag, my parents left the room, but Patrick stayed and watched me.

"Where did you get that hand, Sam?" he asked.

"Do you think I'd tell you after all the trouble you caused, Brat?" I replied.

He shrugged and stared at me. "What else did you get?"

"Lots of stuff—Slime with Eyeballs, Creepy Crawlies, and a spiderweb," I told him. I wanted him to be jealous.

"Hey, neat. I've got a scary record," he said. "Do you want to hear it?"

"No." I stomped off to my room, not wanting to talk to him for another second.

But then I got to thinking: the scary record together with the vacuum-cleaner ghost could be really spooky. That record had some pretty great sound effects on it: doors creaking open, heavy breathing, that sort of thing.

I marched back to Patrick's room and knocked on the door. He opened it cautiously.

"I'll make you a deal," I said, as though I were a TV game show host. "I'll let you see my scary stuff if you let me use your scary record."

His eyes bugged out as only Patrick's eyes can, and he grinned. "Yeah, you got a deal!" he shouted.

I slipped my bag through the crack in the door in exchange for the record.

I narrowed my eyes at him and warned: "Just don't mess anything up."

He shook his head. I could tell he was really scared of me.

"I won't, Samantha," he said. "Promise."

Chapter

4

Letting Patrick look at my party things turned out to be a mistake. He wanted to open up the Slime, and I didn't want it opened until the night of the party. So he followed me around the house all Sunday morning, pleading:

"Please, Sam, let me open the Slime. I want to see the eyeballs. I bet it doesn't really have eyeballs," he whined.

When Patrick whines, he really cranks it up full blast, and my mother usually gets this pained expression on her face and turns to *me*.

"Samantha," she says, "just give him back his toy or whatever it is, and stop causing all this trouble!"

"As if it's all my fault," I complain every time.

"You're the oldest," she tells me.

"Well, he should learn to act right," I tell her.

"You're not his mother," she reminds me. "I am."

That usually ends it right there. What could I say to that?

But this time I knew just what to say.

"Samantha, what is this Slime he's talking about? Why don't you give it to him?"

"Because it's for my party and if I give it to him, he'll put it in his pockets and it'll get all over the laundry," I told her. "*You* remember."

My mom forgets nearly everything, but she does remember laundry disasters. "Oh, is *that* what it was," she said, and I knew she was remembering the time Patrick got Slime on his birthday, and the next day a mysterious, sticky green substance was found in his pockets and throughout the whole load of laundry.

Nobody could forget that.

"I'm going to hide it where nobody can find it," I declared.

"What a good idea!" Mom agreed.

Patrick crossed his arms and glared at me. "I'm *never* letting you borrow my scary record again," he grumbled.

"That's okay, Squirt. I've got it all on tape." I grinned back at him with all my big sisterly power.

"It's not fair," he complained.

I hid my Halloween party things at the bottom of my underwear drawer. I knew Patrick wouldn't look there.

Anyway, my parents got Patrick out of my hair, taking him with them to visit friends, while I got ready to go to the Browns.

As I walked up the path to their front door, I noticed someone had been digging in the flowerbeds. All the flowering plants lay in piles on the cement walkway. Smelling of earth and leaves, Mr. Brown, his normally pale face a little sunburnt, let me into the house.

"You must've been working in the yard," I said.

"Yes. I had to get rid of those dreadful plants," he replied.

"Speaking of plants, Samantha darling," Dr. Brown said as she swooped into the room. She had wound her hair around her head so that it looked like a giant bubble. "Don't water the plants in the kitchen, will you? They're not doing well."

I looked at her in surprise. "Oh, sure, if you say so. I thought plants did better with water."

"Oh, no," she said distractedly, touching the thorny stems of her plants as she started for the door. "Drake is in the laboratory and Lupi is studying somewhere. There's a lot of food in the refrigerator," she added. "Well, we're off. Good night!"

"Good night," I murmured. When they had

gone, the silence settled around me, making me aware of every creak in the floorboards. I went over and looked at the shrunken head which hung by its hair from the mantelpiece.

"Hi, Samantha."

I turned around and saw Lupi standing there with books in her arms. She was wearing her werewolf costume again.

"Hi, Lupi. I was just wondering about your shrunken head," I said. "Where did you get it? It looks so original."

Drake came up beside her. "Oh, it belonged to our last babysitter," he told me with a straight face.

I laughed. "That's a good one. Who would ever think it?"

The two kids stared at me solemnly, so I changed the subject. "How about dinner? Do you like hamburgers?"

They looked at each other. "Hamburgers?"

"Yes, have you got any hamburger meat?" I asked them. When they both gave me puzzled looks, I explained how America's favorite food was made.

"You can use the ground locusts, if you like," Lupi offered, leading the way into the kitchen.

While Lupi put wood in the wood-burning stove, I formed patties with the ground locusts. I wondered why the kids called all their food by such disgusting names. And I couldn't understand why they had such an old-fashioned stove. Then I put the meat on to fry and sent Lupi down to the store for buns.

When she returned, I put her to work setting the table.

"I want my friend Secret to try some," said Drake.

"Okay, set an extra place," I said as I put the burgers on the table.

"We don't have to do *that*," said Lupi. "Secret doesn't eat in front of anybody. She's invisible."

"Hey, I used to have an invisible dog when I was little," I told her. "His name was Fox."

"Really? Where is he now?" she asked, really curious.

What a weird question. Where do most people's imaginary pets go when they grow up? Did she think they followed you into adulthood? "I don't know, I guess he's still around if he's invisible, right?"

She seemed a little troubled, so for her benefit, I said, "Well, once in a while he comes by for a visit."

We sat down. Drake blobbed half a bottle of ketchup on his burger so that I couldn't even see the meat anymore.

"Gee, have some hamburger with your ketchup," I joked.

"I will, thanks," he said, without looking up from his plate.

I had to admit, the hamburgers tasted a little funny: crisp and burned, even though I had cooked them carefully.

"There Secret, it's okay," said Lupi soothingly. She put the plate of food under the table. "As long as we don't look, she'll eat."

"Oh. So how do you like your new house?" I asked them.

Lupi shrugged. "It's okay, but kind of dull. We don't have any ghosts here, except the ones we brought with us. My parents want to import some more. That's what I'm studying about now." She held up a book for me to see, entitled *Ghosts*.

"Oh, that's neat," I said. The book had a leather cover and looked about two hundred years old. "How do you import ghosts?"

Needless to say, these kids had imaginations.

"It's not very easy. You have to encourage them to come," Lupi explained as she pulled a clean plate out from under the table.

"They have to feel comfortable with you," added Drake.

"Wow. Well, let me know when you find one," I said. Obviously Drake and Lupi lived in a world of their own. I guess kids get that way when they spend a lot of time by themselves, and I could see that they were pretty self-sufficient. They were really creative types, I could tell.

After dinner, the kids showed me their bedrooms. Drake had a canopied bed with knives of various sizes hanging down from the overhead canopy. The bed was covered with an animal skin and a moosehead hung on the wall.

"What are all those knives for?" I asked.

"They're from one of my mother's expeditions," Drake answered.

"Oh. Some people collect souvenir spoons," I said. "I guess your mother collects knives."

The children blinked solemnly at me.

"Hey, my uncle Fred has a moosehead like that," I went on. "He keeps it at his cabin in the mountains."

"This one was a friend of my father's," explained Drake. "My father always likes to remember his friends."

I thought having your friends stuffed was a funny way to remember them, and it made me want to giggle. But the moose's serious expression made me think I should be quiet. I knew it was only a stuffed head, but still . . .

Lupi took my hand and I went with her to her bedroom. A cluster of cobwebs laced the doorway, which left me itching.

"Why don't you get rid of those cobwebs?" I asked her.

"Oh, I like them. They're so soft and tickly," she said, leading me to a chair with a big fat stuffed bear sitting in it. Everything looked fairly normal except that the chair had spikes in the seat.

"Who would sit in *that* chair?" I asked, then suddenly realized that I probably sounded like I just stepped out of *The Three Bears*.

"Nobody would, Samantha. Nobody alive, that is," Lupi added. "It's just something my father brought back from one of his trips."

I noticed that she had lots of books, but they all looked very old.

"Do you read a lot?" I asked her.

"Yes."

"Me, too." So we had something in common. Lupi smiled.

I sat down on the bed and heard something rattle. "What's that?"

"You just found my rattlesnake rattler," Lupi told me. "I've been saving them."

"You save them?" I asked.

"Sure," said Lupi. "That one belonged to Samantha, my pet snake."

"I heard about her," I said, shivering.

When I stood in Lupi's or Drake's room, I felt as if I had stepped onto another planet. And the more I learned about the Browns, the stranger I thought they were.

Chapter
5

I didn't think about the Browns much during the next few days. Life got busy. On Thursday, I had a big math test to study for and we had to make arrangements with the principal to use the stage for our haunted house.

"I'll have to check it out with the rest of the faculty, but I think it will be fine," Mr. Owens said. "I like your ideas."

"Thanks," I said. Iris glared at me, because by that point, she thought she had been the one with all the ideas. "We might need some more money."

"Oh?" His eyebrows rose in twin arches of surprise.

It was the same kind of expression my father gets when anyone asks him for money. It must be a universal symbol of alarm.

"This stuff is costing more than we thought. Iris and I have used part of our allowances already," I told him.

"Speak to Ms. Snell about it, Samantha. I'm sure we can work it out so that you get reimbursed," Mr. Owens said.

We didn't get to talk to Ms. Snell right away. She was upset because someone had toilet-papered the girls' bathroom earlier that morning, and it sure wasn't the janitor. Upset was a mild way of putting it—she paced up and down in front of the class, obviously on the warpath.

"I do hope those who did this will come forward to apologize," she said in her best teacher's voice.

Smothered giggles followed. I glanced around, exchanged looks with Iris, and we both figured out who had done it: a group of boys led by Randy Alsip. Randy was about a head shorter than me, but he had just discovered he was cute, so he was really busy being a smart-mouthed pain. He and his friends always sat in the back of the room, pushing and shoving each other. They were so immature. Still, nobody could actually pin the crime on them, so by the end of the day everybody had basically forgotten it.

Once Ms. Snell's lecture was over, I went back to agonizing over the upcoming math test. I was mentally struggling with an equation on the lunch line, when Tommy Deere suddenly popped up next to me.

"How's it going?" he asked.

I jerked out of my trance and stared at him.

He looked uncomfortable. "I mean, with the party and everything."

"Oh, yeah, right," I mumbled. "It's coming along great, just great."

"That's good," Tommy said. "Well, have a nice lunch."

"You, too."

That was it—end of conversation. I met Iris at her table. I could tell just by looking at her that she'd seen Tommy and me talking.

"What did he say? Does he want to join the party committee?" she asked.

"No. He wants a discount ticket," I said sarcastically before biting into my sandwich.

"The nerve!" cried Iris.

"Not so loud," I said, frowning at her. She could be really embarrassing at times. "He asked me how it was going—with the party. I said great, just great. He said have a nice lunch."

"That's amazing," she said.

"Not really, Iris. It's not exactly the world's most interesting conversation," I pointed out.

"It's communication," she insisted. "That's what counts."

As far as I was concerned, Tommy had just been friendly, and I didn't want any more than that. Sometimes I regretted telling Iris things because she quickly blew them out of proportion, and I liked to think about them by myself. I liked what happened between Tommy and me without anybody adding their two cents' worth.

When I went over to the Browns' on Thursday night, I found Drake and Lupi building something.

"It's our project for school," explained Lupi.

It looked like a normal wooden box, except that it had funny jagged spikes sticking out the top.

"What is it?" I asked.

"It's a torture chamber," explained Drake.

"Oh, wow," I muttered. "So what do you do with it?"

They looked at me as if I were crazy.

"We'll show you when it's ready," said Lupi mysteriously.

I watched them attach different-sized stakes to the bottom of the box, wondering what in the world their teacher was going to think of this strange contraption.

"Does your teacher know you're making it?" I asked, thinking that I sounded like Ms. Snell.

"Oh, yes," Lupi said calmly. "It was her idea."

My mouth dropped open.

"You see, we're studying tortures through the ages," explained Drake. "It's fascinating."

I didn't know any kids his age who said "fascinating," nor did I know any kids who studied torture in school.

"Your teacher must be very special," I remarked.

"She is," Lupi replied.

"Well, I'm going to make us some dinner. How about chili dogs?" I suggested.

"I've never had them before, have you, Drake?" Lupi asked her brother. Completely absorbed in his torture chamber, he wagged his head. "They sound interesting," she said.

Obviously they wouldn't have hot dogs in the refrigerator. I would have to figure out a way to get some or plan on something else for dinner.

I went into the kitchen to look in the refrigerator. I was beginning to realize that I'd either have to bring my own food here or eat well before I arrived. As I stared at the ghastly food, something wet suddenly plopped on my head. It was followed by something hard which bounced off my head and plinked to the floor.

I looked down and saw a nail. While I reached down to pick it up, another one plunked down on my head. I touched my hair and my hand came away stained with white stuff. Cautiously, I gave it a sniff. It smelled like house paint!

Then I checked out the ceiling, but I couldn't see any fresh paint up there. So where had it come from?

Just then, another nail plunked down onto the floor next to me, then a hammer!

"What's going on up there?" I shouted indignantly.

"What's wrong?"

Lupi strode through the door, her arms full of wood. "Oh, that's nothing. I see you've met Harry."

"Harry?" I blinked.

"Harry the handyman ghost," she explained, picking up the nails and hammer.

"Come on, Lupi, stop kidding me," I said. "Do you have some guy working on your ceiling or something?"

I squinted up at the flat white ceiling, but saw nothing.

"Samantha, Harry is a real ghost. We brought him with us from our old home. He's really clumsy and he's always dropping things," Lupi said with utmost seriousness. "He also loses everything, so you have to put his tools in a place where he can find them again."

"He sounds like my mother," I muttered. But this was getting interesting, so I just had to go along with it. "Where do you put his tools so he can find them?" I asked.

"Well, since he's working right about here," she said, forming a circle on the floor with her foot. "I'd say we should leave them right here."

"In the middle of the floor?" I cried. "We might trip on them."

Lupi shrugged. "Sure. But so will Harry. If he doesn't find his tools, he makes a terrible noise."

"Like what?"

Lupi took a deep breath and let out a shrill, high-pitched shriek. "Eeeeeeeeeeeeeeeeek!"

I clamped my hands over my ears. "Sorry I asked," I told her. "Do you have an aspirin?"

"An aspirin?" Lupi looked confused again. Her big blue eyes opened wide.

I explained that an aspirin was a pill to take away headaches.

"Oh, if you have a headache, we have just the thing for you. Come with me," Lupi urged. I followed her to the laboratory, where little beakers and test tubes bubbled with strange substances.

"Sit here," she ordered, pointing to a funny seat that almost looked like a bean-bag chair. Above it hung a big vise like you usually see in workshops.

I hesitated. "Don't worry, Samantha," Lupi

said encouragingly. "We won't hurt you. Just relax while I get Drake."

Nervously, I sat down, sinking into the depths of the chair. I had the sudden sensation that the chair was swallowing me.

"Hey, what's with this chair!" I cried.

"The chair won't hurt you," explained Lupi. "It just wants you to feel comfortable."

"I'll take your word for it," I replied.

A minute later she came back with Drake, smiling as though he were a miniature doctor.

"Don't be afraid, Samantha," he said. "You'll be better in no time. Our mother always does this for us when we have head-aches."

"This is a long way from an aspirin," I joked.

They didn't answer. Drake said, "Okay, put your head back, and I'm going to close the vise on it."

I did as I was told. "Are you sure this won't hurt?" I asked.

"No, you'll just feel a little pressure on your ears," said Lupi quietly.

Sure enough, I felt the cold metal tighten around my ears, and a cold feeling tightened up in my stomach. What if they squeezed too hard?

Drake started chanting: "Squeeze the head, press the brain, until Samantha feels no pain."

He chanted repeatedly, and I can't remember the exact words, but that's what it sounded like to me.

The vise tightened around my ears, squashing them to the sides of my head. Drake had his eyes closed and seemed to be off in another world. Wow, I thought, what if he completely spaced out on me? I began to worry about my safety.

"Hey, Drake, I hate to interrupt, but don't you think this has gone too far?" I yelled above his chanting. "I mean, it's kind of tight, you know?"

His eyes fluttered open and he shut up. "Okay, you're probably ready then. I'll let you out."

With that, he cranked the vise loose, and I freed my head from it. My ears tingled. Boy, was I glad that was over!

Lupi pressed her hand into mine. "How do you feel now, Samantha?"

"Do you still have a headache?" asked Drake.

"Headache?" I glanced questioningly from one to the other, and then laughed. "Wow, I forgot about it. I guess it worked! I don't have a headache anymore."

"See? We told you so!" They looked pleased with themselves. .

I stood up, feeling my ears and my head for signs of damage. I guess I was so concerned about whether my head was going to be pressed into chopped meat that I forgot about my headache. Or maybe there was something magical about the vise. Who knows?

Lupi and Drake led the way back through the house.

"Oh, look, Harry found his tools," exclaimed Lupi.

I glanced down at the kitchen floor. Sure enough, the hammer and nails had disappeared. I touched the top of my hair, feeling the paint which had dried to a hard mass.

"I'll have to wash my hair," I sighed. "Harry dropped paint on me."

"You'll have to excuse him," said Drake. "He's such a clumsy ghost, you never know what he's going to do next. You'll just have to stay out of his way, Samantha."

"How can I do that if I don't know where he is?" I asked.

"That's a good point," said Lupi. "But you get to know where ghosts are after a while."

"Yeah, right," I said. Lupi made it all sound so logical.

But then, these kids had a wild explanation for everything!

Chapter
6

If I thought Harry the handyman ghost was weird, I was in for a big surprise. Harry was nothing compared to what came next.

I babysat for the Brown children on Friday evening, too, because Dr. and Mr. Brown had to go to a special "scientific convention." They wore their antique clothes again, and I wondered what kind of a convention would expect such weirdly dressed guests. If they were in the theater or movies, that kind of strangeness would seem more normal.

But they weren't in the movies, so who were they and why were they so different? *What* were they? Not knowing this made me a little nervous.

I had brought some hot dogs, a can of chili, buns, and chocolate ice cream in order to introduce the kids to this all-American meal.

(I still couldn't believe that anyone living in America in the twentieth century had never eaten a hot dog!) I was in the kitchen, digging around in a cupboard for suitable pots and pans. I saw a lot of ants and various other bugs crawling around freely. I had asked Dr. Brown about this problem and whether she wanted me to get bug killer or something, but she had said, "Oh, no, Samantha. They're friendly," in a very serious tone, so what could I say to that?

Anyway, I found a pot and a pan while brushing ants and assorted flying bugs off my arms. Wow, they gave me the creeps, and I came away from the experience itching like crazy. They might be friendly, but they sure were annoying. I didn't know how the Browns could stand it, but then they seemed so in tune with this environment.

Lupi and Drake were outside working on their torture chamber. Kimmie was in Lupi's room playing. I put the hot dogs and chili on to cook.

When the front door opened, I expected the two kids to walk in for dinner, but instead an odd-smelling breeze moved through the house. It smelled like dirt and rotten oranges. Let's face it, I could never tell what Lupi and Drake were going to get into next—and Kimmie was staying tonight as well—so I sighed and pulled the chili off the heat.

The smell got stronger, and I thought it was going to knock me out. Then I heard something odd—like palm leaves being dragged across the floor—swish, swish, then footsteps —thud, thud.

I turned around. A horrible wrapped-up figure stood before me, completely covered with mud and leaves! It was wrapped up like a mummy; only one sinister eye stared from a space in its torn wrapping. The eye blinked, but didn't flinch from my face. I stared at the apparition, my mouth hanging open, fear filling me so fast I probably suffered brain damage—all this before I screamed. The figure advanced toward me. Then I screamed and screamed until Lupi and Drake ran inside to see what was going on. Kimmie appeared in the doorway, blinking at me in surprise.

"Oh, Samantha, it's nothing, really," I heard Lupi saying through my screams. "We forgot to tell you about Uncle Tompkins. He's really harmless."

"Calm down, Samantha," Drake was saying. "Let us introduce you to Uncle Tompkins. He . . . er . . . lives in the backyard and he comes inside once in a while."

"He lives in the backyard?" I squeaked, my ice-cold hands pressed against my face.

"In a manner of speaking," said Lupi.

Uncle Tompkins' stare did not waver. I

wished he'd stop looking at me like that. And the way he smelled was enough to kill a horse.

Trembling, I said, "Pleased to meet you."

Uncle Tompkins extended his hand for me to shake. Terrified, I glanced from Lupi to Drake, and they looked completely calm—as if this were an everyday occurrence. Well, was it? Boy, I was glad I wasn't here every day!

"I think Uncle Tompkins wants to shake hands," Drake urged.

Of course he wanted to shake hands. I nodded, smiled, and extended my hand to this mummy creature.

The wrapped hand grasped mine. It felt like material covering stone, as though the person underneath the wrapping were dead. Dead!— that's what mummies were—dead people! Samantha, where have you been? I heard myself screaming inside. As the smell of dirt and rotten oranges engulfed me, I closed my eyes, ready to faint.

At that moment, Uncle Tompkins let my hand go.

"Samantha, are you all right?" asked Drake.

Lupi shook me gently. I opened my eyes. Uncle Tompkins had gone, but I could still hear the funny swish, swish, thud, thud of his footsteps as he shambled out of the house.

"Was he really here?" I stammered.

"Oh, yes. Our father is very concerned about our relatives," Lupi explained. "He believes our strength is in our numbers, so he wants us to stay together."

I said something like, "That's very nice." My hand and the whole kitchen smelled like Uncle Tompkins. I asked Lupi if I could wash.

"Sure," she said.

"That . . . smell," I said. "What do you do about it?"

"Oh, I hardly notice it anymore. Here, this works really well." Lupi handed me some shiny red leaves which looked a little like poison ivy or poison oak. "If you rub these on your hands, the smell will go away."

As though in a trance, I rubbed the leaves on my hands. And just as Lupi had said, the smell went away.

Trying to push the incident out of my mind, I went back to the stove and reheated the dinner. Lupi perched Kimmie at her place.

"Hungry!" she cried, banging her spoon against the tabletop.

"It's coming, Kimmie," I said, but I was fumbling with everything. I showed Drake how the hot dogs fitted in the buns, but my hands shook so badly I couldn't carry the plates. He helped me bring the food to the table.

"That looks good!" Kimmie cried, clapping her hands delightedly.

I noticed one of the hot dogs missing from the plate Drake carried.

"I'm sure I put four hot dogs on that plate," I said.

"Kimmie has hers already. She beamed it over because she couldn't wait," Lupi said, laughing.

"She did *what?*" I stared at Kimmie's plate.

"Kimmie can move things just by thinking about it. It's very convenient," Drake explained.

"I guess it is," I said thoughtfully. "Is she telepathic?"

"Telekinetic," he corrected me.

"That's wonderful," I replied, wondering what it would be like to move stuff around at will. It had its high points, I'm sure. Just think, if I were like Kimmie, I could move my little brother to darkest Africa whenever I wanted.

Still, after Uncle Tompkins, I didn't think very much could upset me ever again. I sat at the dinner table with the Brown kids, eating a normal American dinner of chili dogs, hoping to introduce chocolate ice cream for dessert. Nothing could be more normal, could it?

I could almost forget that nightmare scene in the kitchen earlier. I could've dreamt the whole scene. I mean, it would make sense—when I opened my eyes again, Uncle Tompkins wasn't there. Kaput. Gone. I heard him shuffling away, but then that could've been anything, right? After all, if Kimmie could make things move around the room, then maybe the other kids could make things appear that weren't really there.

But I knew I had smelled, touched, and seen Uncle Tompkins. He was unbearably real.

After dinner, we moved some dead plants so that we could hang up some of the children's Halloween decorations.

"Don't you think your mother would like to throw these plants out?" I suggested to Lupi.

"Oh, no!" she cried in horror. (Lupi didn't seem horrified by very much.) "Those are my mother's pets."

What could I say? Obviously, getting rid of the plants was a dead issue.

Lupi and Drake had some spider-shaped designs made from a black rubbery material that they stuck on the windows. Then they brought out some skulls and put candles in them.

"Those skulls are great," I remarked. "Did you make them yourselves? I remember one year I made one from a model, and it glowed in the dark."

Drake stared at me. "These aren't models, Samantha. These are real skulls. Look at the detail."

I looked at the skulls carefully. They were much more detailed than my glow-in-the-dark skull.

"Where did you get them?" I asked, although by that time I really didn't want to know.

"Our Aunt Amelia is in the grave-robbing business," Lupi explained.

"Some of them have been in our family for centuries," added Drake.

I went home around eleven o'clock—exhausted. I wanted to talk to Iris because I felt desperate to hear a normal voice, but I couldn't call her at eleven o'clock at night.

I got ready for bed and turned off the light, but I couldn't sleep. I turned on the light again, got up and checked that nothing except clothes was in any of the closets. Satisfied, I crawled back into bed, turned on my radio, and closed my eyes. Finally, I guess I must have fallen asleep, because I woke up with a start.

My window had flung open and a stiff breeze blew into the room. I got up and locked it, shivering with fright and cold.

I wished I had somebody I could talk to. Every time I closed my eyes I saw Uncle Tompkins' blank eye stuck on me. And my secret knowledge lay heavily on my chest, like a cold mummy hand.

Chapter
7

"Iris, I have to talk to you," I said urgently—after a sleepless, haunted night.

"Come on over. I just washed my hair," she said.

I hopped on my bicycle and rode over to her house. I liked Iris' house. It was on a corner and several shade trees grew in the front and back yards, and when we were little, Iris and I built a treehouse in one of them. From that viewpoint, we could spy on the whole neighborhood.

When I rang the doorbell, Iris answered with a towel wrapped turban-style around her head.

"Samantha, what's wrong with you?" she asked right away.

Iris always knew when I was angry, unhappy, sick, delirious, or ecstatic. I could always tell with her, too.

"It's the Browns," I blurted out. "They're so weird. They don't seem quite human."

I followed Iris upstairs to her room. I went into the whole thing about how Dr. Brown didn't want me to water her plants. Then I said, "And I had this strange dream over there . . ."

"You fell asleep there?"

"Well, no, I mean yes," I stumbled, not wanting to tell her that Uncle Tompkins had happened in broad daylight when I was wide awake. "I mean I was daydreaming, I guess."

"That makes more sense," she agreed.

I told her the dream, but she thought it was crazy. Who wouldn't?

"But what about the plants? I offered to throw them out, but Lupi said no, you can't do that—they're her mother's pets," I went on.

"Lupi? Her name is Lupi? That's weird," Iris said, shrugging. "I don't know about the plants, Sam. I mean, maybe they just don't take good care of their plants. My Aunt May has a house full of dead plants. Did I ever tell you about her?"

"No, I must have missed that one. I thought maybe that was the way the Browns were, too," I replied. "But they treat plants as though they *should* be dead."

Iris shrugged. "I don't know what to tell

you. I've never heard of anything like this. I think you're imagining things. Want a Coke?"

"Sure," I said, following her into the kitchen and then back to her room. "Then Drake said that the little one, their cousin Kimmie, is telekinetic. Do you know what that means?"

"She's got a disease?" Iris guessed.

"No. She can move things around without touching them," I told her.

Iris leaned over and took a good look at me. "Oh, so you mean she can send the dishwasher flying over to a different corner of the room, just because she thinks of it?"

"Sort of," I responded sheepishly.

Her expression changed. I knew she wasn't taking any of this seriously. "Sam, you look really weird," she told me. "I think these kids have really wild imaginations. They're just pulling your leg. You know, you're really pretty gullible."

"Yeah, you're right. They really do have wild imaginations," I agreed, but that wasn't all. All of a sudden, I knew that I couldn't tell Iris everything, and it felt funny to withhold information from my best friend. I even felt sad.

I rode home on my bike, feeling as if I were alone in the world. I mean, what I had experienced at the Browns was so weird that sometimes I wasn't sure even I believed it.

I leaned my bike up against the garage door

and went straight to my room to find my dictionary. It's funny, I seem to know a lot of words but I don't know many definitions. When people ask me what a word means, it usually takes me a half hour to explain it to them, when it would take two minutes with a dictionary.

I thumbed through it until I came to the word "telekinesis." "The apparent production of motion in objects (as by a spiritualistic medium) without contact or other physical means."

I slumped back in my chair with the book open on my lap. Could Kimmie be a "spiritualistic medium?" I asked myself. The idea was totally loony, just like everything else lately. Whenever you saw mediums on a TV show, they were always adults—not little kids just learning to talk.

Maybe Kimmie was the product of some scientific experiment. Maybe she was a mutant. As a result, she could move things around by thinking about them. Just think, if she got really mad, she could hurl a piano in your face!

I shuddered. I went into the living room to look in the encyclopedia for more information.

Just as I passed the couch, something jumped out from behind it.

"Rahhh!" it yelled.

I was blasted with this image of a face with

blood dripping over bared teeth, stringy black hair hanging over mad red eyes. I screamed and screamed and screamed.

A hand reached up from under its cloak and ripped off the grotesque face. Patrick stood there grinning at me, twirling the face mask on his index finger as though he had just done something wonderful.

"It's only a mask, Sam," he crowed.

In one split second, I zoomed from scream mode into a full rage. "You little brat!" I yelled. "Don't you ever do that to me again, do you hear?"

He giggled. "But you *were* really scared, weren't you?" he insisted.

"Get lost!" I yelled again, and ran after him until he started screaming for his mommy.

Chapter
8

"We want to buy more of the food you like," Lupi told me on Sunday, the next time I babysat. "Will you take us shopping?"

"Sure. Don't you shop around here?"

"No," she said. "My mother shops somewhere across town."

I couldn't imagine where and I probably wouldn't know the place if she told me. Anyway, I had told myself I was going to ignore their strangeness this time.

We went to Tommy Deere's father's store. Actually, it was called "Bud's," which I guess was Tommy's father's name.

Everything went pretty well at first. When we entered the store, Lupi looked around tentatively, then she started to walk down the aisles, touching things on the shelves. I just let her go ahead, figuring she was old enough to know what she was doing. I glimpsed Tommy behind the cold-cuts machine, cutting up what looked like a lump of ham. I watched how carefully he pushed the ham against the blade, thinking that he really had a way with cold cuts.

"Samantha, what's this?" Lupi asked me, pulling a can of Spaghetti-Os off the shelf.

"It's a prepared food, made of ground meat and spaghetti," I explained. I sounded like a kindergarten teacher on a field trip. "I've never eaten it."

"Can we buy some?" she asked me.

"I guess so." Dr. Brown had left me money for the children's dinner.

"Oh, look at this!" cried Drake. In an instant, he had lunged at the ketchup display, knocking the bottles down like dominoes. They rolled off the shelf and along the narrow wooden floor, bumping up against cans of olive oil.

Tommy's father craned his neck into the aisle to see what we were doing, so I quickly replaced the bottles.

"We need all the ketchup," Drake insisted.

"You've got some at home," I reminded him.

"But we need more," he said fiercely.

What was wrong with him? He had set his jaw in a grim line and I couldn't understand why he was so uptight.

"We'll buy one more bottle, but that's all," I said firmly.

At that moment, something fluttered past me, missing my ear by a hair. At first I thought it was a bird, but then when I saw the funny webbed wingspread, I shrieked.

Another shopper saw it at the same time and screamed, too.

"Mr. Deere, you have bats in your store," someone else cried indignantly.

"Mrs. Elworth, calm down; we've never had bats in *this* store," Mr. Deere said.

"Lupi, you shouldn't bring her to the store," Drake told his sister. "Samantha, Lupi brought her pet in her jacket."

Lupi stood with her jacket slung awkwardly over her shoulder, smiling.

Just then the bat let out a shriek. I glanced in the direction of the noise. The bat had perched itself precariously on top of some cereal boxes. The boxes were arranged in a pyramid, close to the ceiling. One false move and the whole thing . . .

I saw the pyramid of boxes cave in and start to tumble. I closed my eyes. I don't know why not looking seemed like my first reaction, but I felt totally helpless.

"Lupi, do something!" I hissed.

"I can't do anything!" she cried. "He won't listen now. He's scared, poor thing."

Boxes cascaded down from the top shelves,

bonking customers on the tops of their heads. But that wasn't enough. Having done that damage, the bat flew on to the canned food display and knocked down soups and baked beans and tuna, so that customers had to dodge the flying merchandise. Then he went on to knock down jars of coffee and bags of sugar and flour, which burst open when they hit the floor, leaving a sea of whiteness. Lupi and Drake stared at the wreckage in amazement. People screamed their heads off.

"What's going on here!"

"Stop it this instant!"

"I'm calling the police!"

"This is outrageous!" Wiping his hands on his apron, Tommy's father charged toward me, his face turning redder and redder, ready to kill. "I want you out of my store, do you hear me? Out! Right now!" He pointed in the direction of the door.

"But, Mr. Deere, we were just . . ." I stammered.

"Didn't you hear me, young lady! You come in here and knock things down, bring a bat into my store and scare my customers half to death. I'll see that you pay for this. Now if you don't get out of here, right this minute, I'm going to call the police and have you arrested. Do you understand me now?"

Trembling, I nodded my head. Just then, I realized that the cold-cuts machine had stopped. I lifted my eyes and saw Tommy glaring at me, wearing the same expression as his father.

I wanted to sink through the floor.

"Lupi and Drake, go outside, please," I said.

Lupi motioned to the bat, who left his perch on the shelf and flew out the door after her. Then she quickly tucked him inside her jacket.

"Aren't we going to buy dinner?" Drake wanted to know as I started out the door.

"No, we're not eating dinner," I snapped at him.

He looked at me as if I were a stranger. I'd always been so nice before. But this was no time to be nice.

At that moment, I couldn't think about food. Food was the last thing in the world I wanted to think or hear about. I didn't care if I ever ate again.

When we got back to the Browns' house, I collapsed on the couch. The telephone started to ring, and I heard Lupi answer.

"Samantha, it's for you," she said sweetly.

I didn't smile at her. All the way home, they had been tiptoeing around me because I was so mad.

"Hello?"

"Samantha, what is the meaning of this?"

That tone of voice could only have belonged to my mother. Obviously she knew all about the store caper. She had had a call from Mr. Deere.

"A bat? Samantha, are you out of your mind? Bats carry diseases. What is a child doing with a bat, would you please tell me that?"

"It's not *her* bat, Mom, it just followed us to the store," I lied. What was I supposed to do? There was no way I could tell her the truth.

"A bat does not follow children to the store like a dog follows children—unless, of course, it's rabid." Suddenly, my mother shrieked into the phone. I covered my ears. I'd heard just about enough shrieking for one day. "Samantha, do you realize that a bat that flies in daylight is usually rabid? Did you know that?"

"Well, now that you mention it . . ."

"Samantha, did the bat bite anybody?" she demanded.

"No, Mom. It just knocked over cereal boxes and stuff," I assured her.

"Are you absolutely sure?" she persisted.

"Mom, I'm sure someone would've mentioned it if they'd been bitten," I said.

"Listen, Mr. Deere wants to be reimbursed for the damages. And you'll have to pay for them, I'm afraid."

"Don't worry," I said.

I gulped. There was nothing worse than having to part with hard-earned money, unless it was the humiliation of having to part with it in order to pay for trashing Tommy's father's store.

I hung up and went back into the living room.

"Samantha, is everything okay?" Lupi asked, her big blue eyes wide with concern.

"No, everything is not okay," I grumbled. "I'm in big trouble." I explained that I would have to pay for the damage done in the store.

"We'll speak to our mother about it," she said. "I'm sure she can arrange something."

"You don't have to do that," I said quickly, not sure I wanted any more of their help.

Drake opened his coat. The inside lining sported many pockets, all stuffed with bottles of ketchup! It was a professional thief's coat!

"What are you doing with all that ketchup?" I demanded. "Don't you know that's stealing?"

He looked at me blankly.

"Now we'll have to return all the ketchup to Mr. Deere, too, unless we pay for it," I explained.

"Let's pay for it," he urged. "I just couldn't bear coming home without dinner."

"We can have macaroni and cheese for dinner. Ketchup is not dinner," I replied.

"It is to me," Drake insisted. He stuck his lower lip out in a pout.

Rolling my eyes in exasperation, I noticed the bat perched in the rafters. It folded its wings up so you could hardly tell it was there. I wondered if it had rabies. And I wondered what I was going to do with a thief on my hands. I could always quit this babysitting job—even though I was generally very dependable and loyal.

I looked back at Drake's coat. He had taken so many bottles of ketchup, Mr. Deere would think the kid was some kind of nut. My reputation was already in ruins, and this would make me look like a complete idiot. But there was only one thing I could do. I had to take the ketchup back.

Finally, I sighed and said, "Drake, put all those bottles in a paper bag. We're going back to the store."

His eyes lit up. "Why? Do we get to keep the ketchup?"

"No. We don't have enough money. But you have to return it and explain," I told him.

This time, I made sure that we left the bat at home. And I coached Drake on what to say to Mr. Deere about the ketchup.

On the way to the store, I thought about running away. Maybe my parents could send me to boarding school so that I would never have to see Tommy or Davis Junior High again.

Mr. Deere saw us approaching and ran outside. "You're not coming back in here!" he cried, shaking his fist.

I marched forward and dropped the bag at his feet. "We're returning this," I explained. "The boy is from another country and doesn't understand our customs."

Drake smiled sweetly. "Dee-beelzedoop," he said with his hand outstretched—as though he wanted to shake Mr. Deere's hand. "Dee-munch-litzee."

I stared at him. That wasn't what I had coached him to say at all! I knew he was trying to pretend he was from another country, but what language *was* that? I hoped it was some kind of apology.

Mr. Deere peered in the bag. "All this ketchup?" He looked at me questioningly.

I shrugged like I didn't understand it either, which was true.

A few customers passed us to get into the store, and Mr. Deere picked up the bag and glared at us. "All right, go. I never want to see you kids again!"

In that instant, I happened to glimpse Tommy staring at me again.

I turned away from the store and walked in the other direction, with Lupi and Drake close behind me.

I was thinking: I should quit right now before anything else happens—except that when they weren't ruining my life or scaring me, I liked the kids. I had to take that into consideration, but still, making a public spectacle in front of a boy you like, trashing his father's store and having a giant debt on top of it all was a little more than I had counted on.

But then I suddenly remembered: I couldn't quit. This was the best-paying job in town, and now I had to get the money to pay back Tommy's father!

Chapter
=9=

The next morning, Monday, I woke up feeling miserable. My throat felt sore, my face was on fire, and when I climbed out of bed I nearly fell down from dizziness.

My mom came zooming in with her trusty thermometer, and found that I had a 102-degree temperature. I don't know why mothers get a kick out of leaving a thermometer in your mouth until it's digging into the back of your gums.

"Did that bat bite you?" she asked worriedly.

"No, Mom," I said with a sigh.

"Well, I'm calling the doctor anyway. You could have rabies, you know. In any case, I pronounce you too sick to go to school," she said, shaking the thermometer down from its red-hot height.

I thought she was overreacting, but I wasn't about to argue. Nobody was ever happier to be sick than I was. I'd been wondering how I could possibly go to school and face Tommy after what had happened. I'd gone to bed thinking about it and I woke up thinking about it. But now I could stay home until all the excitement had blown over. Maybe Tommy would forget by the time I got back to school. Or maybe my sickness could be a weird strain that would change my appearance so much that no one would recognize me. I could create a whole new identity and Tommy would never have to know. He'd just wonder where that crazy Samantha Slade had disappeared to.

Or maybe he'd be just as glad as I was that I didn't have to go to school. Who needs to be faced with an embarrassment?

We went to see Dr. Macklin, who assured my mother that I did not have rabies, just the flu. So we went back home and Mom made sure I was safely tucked in bed. After all the usual "drink your orange juice, take your aspirin, make sure you rest" fussing that mothers are universally famous for, Mom finally left for work. I was grateful to her for not bringing up the subject of the store incident. I was sure that if she did, I'd have a relapse or go into a coma, or even start frothing at the mouth. But I think she got so worried about me that she almost forgot I had made a public nuisance of myself less than twenty-four hours before.

Then I started to wonder whether I'd gotten sick from eating something over at the Browns'. Suddenly I wasn't so sure they were joking about the menu. Seriously, what if I'd really eaten locusts and tarantula legs? Imagine what that could do to a normal American stomach!

I fell asleep for a while, then got up to find something to read. I found a dog-eared copy of *The Man of a Thousand Faces,* a biography of Lon Chaney, the horror actor. According to the book, he was a master of monster makeup and could create any image he wanted. I remembered seeing him in *The Wolfman* and *The Phantom of the Opera.*

I must've slept for most of the day, because when the phone rang, it woke me up. It was Iris, just home from school. I started to tell her about what had happened in Bud's, but she cut me off.

"Samantha, I already heard about it from my mother who heard it from Mrs. Simms. She even said there was a bat in the store. Is that true?" Iris asked.

"Well, sort of . . ." I answered nervously.

"It sounds awful, but I'm sure there's more to the story than what Mrs. Simms told my mother," she went on.

"There is—lots more," I said, closing my

eyes. In a feverish haze, I remembered Lupi and her pet bat.

"I want to hear about it, but no matter what happens, Sam, I'll still be your friend and everything," Iris said quickly.

"Gee, thanks, Iris," I replied, feeling wretched. Then I told her my version of the story.

"You'll never be able to go to school again," she declared. "Do you realize how serious this is?"

"Thanks for the vote of confidence," I said. "You really don't think Tommy will forget what happened?"

"How could anyone forget you making a complete idiot of yourself and destroying an entire store?" she pointed out.

"But it wasn't my fault!" I cried. My head was spinning.

"Who cares? The fact is, you were there, breaking up the store, and the whole neighborhood knows it. They might even put an article in the paper about it," she said.

"Oh, no!" I groaned and dropped the phone. I heard Iris' voice, sounding kind of unreal, squeaking at me from the receiver. "Sam, are you there?" An article in the paper would ruin me. Finally, I picked up the receiver again. "Iris, don't say anything to anybody else about this, okay?"

"Okay."

"And if anybody asks you if you've talked to me, and they want to know what I said about it, tell them it wasn't my fault," I told her.

"You know I'll stick up for you, Sam. Do you think I want to see my friend become a public outcast?" she asked.

"No, I just want people to forget about it as soon as possible," I said. "I wish there were some kind of serum you could give a whole town so the population would get amnesia."

"Great. Can you just see sixty thousand people forgetting their car keys?" Iris started cracking up. "Forgetting to pick up their kids from football practice? Forgetting to go to work?"

"All right, all right. It was just an idea."

"Did I ever tell you about my Uncle Horace —the time he ran the car into the police station at one o'clock in the morning?" Iris asked me.

"No, you didn't," I replied, laughing. "What happened to *this* relative?"

"He got a ticket. But the worst thing about it is that nobody *ever* forgot it," she said in a low voice.

"I get the point, Iris," I moaned.

"Good luck. That's all I can say right now," she said, and hung up.

I stayed home for two days, reading and wishing I were Lon Chaney and could create at least one of his thousand faces. Of course, it didn't do any good, and at the end of my sickness, I still looked the same.

I liked the idea of amnesia. I'd seen a couple of soap operas where somebody got amnesia and couldn't remember their own husbands, then went off and married somebody else. That was almost as dramatic as what had happened to me, I thought.

On Wednesday, my mom said I was well enough to go to school.

"Are you sure?" I asked. "I still feel a little dizzy."

"I think you'll survive," she said calmly. "I'll write a note excusing you from phys. ed."

There was no arguing my way out of that one. I thought about wearing a bag over my head, but that would probably have attracted more attention than I needed.

"Samantha, we've paid Mr. Deere for the damage done to his store," my mother said. "Your father and I talked about it, and we decided that you can pay us back out of your babysitting money. We can work out a payment schedule later."

"Gee, thanks, Mom," I told her, but I wasn't really happy about it.

When I got to school, Tommy was standing at the homeroom door. There was no way around him—I had to walk right past him to get into the room.

I said, "hi," but he didn't respond. He

turned away! My heart sank into my sneakers. I moved past him quickly, hot tears stinging my eyes. After I sat down, I noticed that every eye was on me. It was worse than I had imagined. He must've told everyone what I'd done—or what he thought I'd done. It didn't matter now. As far as everyone was concerned, I was guilty of trashing his father's store.

Iris shot me a sympathetic look. She'd seen the whole thing. I tried to smile back at her, but I had to look away. Sympathy has a terrible effect on me. If I were ready to die, the last thing anyone should do for me is show me any sympathy. I think I'd like a joke better. "Oh, poor Samantha" causes me to burst into tears. Someone hugging me has an even worse effect. Just everybody stay away, please. In my case, misery does not love company.

At lunch, I told Iris I was going out on the front lawn to do some thinking. She frowned.

"Samantha, are you all right? Are you sure you don't want me to come with you?" She put her arm around my shoulder and lowered her voice to a whisper. "Look, I know things look pretty bad, but try not to worry about all those dummies in there."

"Thanks, Iris. I just want to think things over on my own for a few minutes," I said. "But you just gave me a great idea. We can dress up dummies as dead people and have them lying around the haunted house."

"Super!" declared Iris. "My mom can supply the dummies."

That may sound ridiculous, but Iris' mother works at a department store as a buyer, and she can get all the dress dummies she wants.

Even after such a great idea, I only felt a little better. I went off by myself, which I don't do very often. I sat down under a bunch of trees where nobody ever sits because the squirrels drop nuts on your head.

It seemed like ever since the incident at Tommy's store, I'd been telling everybody it wasn't my fault. And it wasn't. I didn't do anything wrong. The fact that the kids got out of hand was, well, too bad, but then nobody except me knew what monsters the Brown kids were. (I wasn't sure yet, either.) Then I thought of Tommy standing there behind the cold cuts, staring at me. He didn't say a word, just stared.

It occurred to me that he didn't stick up for me, like Iris would've done. He just let me suffer all that humiliation all by myself. With all those customers screaming, a bat flying around, ketchup bottles all over the place, everything a big mess—he never once stepped in to help me.

Maybe he was scared to speak up in front of his dad, but he should've known that I didn't mean to wreck the store. He just looked at it in black and white: "Before she came in with those kids, everything was fine, but now look at it." He agreed with his father, right? Worse, everyone knew about the store incident—customers probably went home and told their kids. And when I walked into class, everybody started looking at me. Tommy must've told a great story while I was absent.

I stood up and brushed off my jeans. I was mad, and when I got mad, I felt better. Because I knew Tommy was wrong for letting his father kick me out of the store. He was a big chicken. He never even thanked me for bringing back the ketchup. The kids and I could've taken off for California with twenty bottles of ketchup, never to be seen again. He ought to be thankful, that's all I could say. We could've been a lot worse.

Chapter
═══10═══

After school on Thursday, Iris and I went to buy some fake blood for our dummies and then began working on the dead bodies. We dressed them in some of our parents' ratty painting clothes and put wigs on them. Iris' mother had brought home a big selection of wigs. We wrapped one of the bodies up in torn sheets so that it looked like a mummy, and it reminded me so much of Uncle Tompkins that it made me shiver.

I went over to the Browns' to babysit that evening. Lupi and Drake seemed happy to see me. I was pleased—at least somebody liked having me around.

"Samantha, we're so excited!" Drake exclaimed. He was usually the quiet, mysterious one, so I was surprised to hear him so talkative. "Our parents bought some movies from the video center and I'm setting up the TV now. Come on, you'll love them."

"Sounds like fun," I agreed. I guess there isn't anybody who doesn't love the movies.

Lupi was already sitting in the den. "Okay, ready, set? This is my favorite movie."

Drake set up the VCR and we all sat back to watch. The movie was old, in black-and-white, and the words "King Kong" flashed on the screen.

"Hey, is this the original *King Kong?*" I asked.

"I don't know if it's the first," Lupi said. "It's the one with Fay Wray."

"That's probably the very first one. It's a classic," I said.

We sat silently watching for a while in the dark. Lupi passed around a bag of crunchy things that actually tasted pretty good.

When the man that Fay Wray was in love with came on the screen, Lupi said, "You know, he's nothing compared to King Kong. He's just so ordinary and he smiles at all the wrong times. What do you think, Samantha?"

"Well, I don't remember whether King Kong smiles at all," I replied.

"He does—just watch!" she cried. "But don't you think the man is ordinary?"

"I don't know—uh, he's just a man, I guess." This was a weird conversation.

Finally, King Kong came onto the scene. I started to laugh.

"What's so funny?" demanded Lupi.

"He's so mechanical. You can see how unreal he is," I said.

"I think he's very real," she insisted. "Look at his expression. Look how much in love he is with the girl. It's a wonderful romance. She's frightened, but she gets really attached to him because he protects her."

"Not like Tommy," I blurted out.

"Who?" Lupi asked distractedly.

"Oh, nobody you know," I replied, turning my attention back to the screen.

"You mean Tommy in the store—the boy behind the counter," she said.

"I didn't know you noticed him."

"I noticed him," she said simply, "watching you."

"You did? Really?" This was news to me.

"Hey, Samantha, watch this," she urged. "This is the best part."

"Yeah, will you two be quiet?" asked Drake. He lay on the floor with his chin cupped in his hands and his eyes glued to the screen.

King Kong started to carry Fay into the jungle, and she was screaming her head off and driving me crazy.

"I hope I don't sound like that when I scream," I said.

"She screams much more than you, Samantha," Drake added, giggling.

"Nobody screams more than Samantha," insisted Lupi, winking at her brother. "Not even the last babysitter."

"The last . . . babysitter?" I stammered. I only had one image of the "last babysitter": a shrunken head on the mantelpiece. "She's not screaming now."

"No, she's all screamed out." Drake laughed.

"All right, you guys," I grumbled, but I could see how much they enjoyed teasing me about this shrunken head.

"But King Kong doesn't mind—he loves her even though she makes all that noise," Lupi said dreamily.

"Lupi, you're acting like King Kong is really romantic. He's just a monster," I reminded her.

She looked at me blankly. "He's a hero, Samantha. He just might not be your type."

"Gee, I guess not. What happened to those crunchy things?" I asked, watching the girl fall asleep in the palm of King Kong's hand.

"You mean the Dragon Krispies," corrected Drake.

"I suppose so. They're delicious," I said.

"I'll get some more," he offered, and left the room.

Lupi started sniffling when King Kong stood on top of the Empire State Building, catching planes. And she cried when he finally died and the girl ran up and sobbed on his huge chest.

"It's so sad," she whimpered. "How can they make movies like this without crying?"

Next we watched *King Kong Meets Godzilla,* which also upset Lupi because she liked both monsters so much, she wanted both to win the fight at the end.

"It doesn't matter if one of them loses," Drake told her practically. "Both of them can come back for another movie, or they can be like Uncle Tompkins."

"Uncle Tompkins!" I exclaimed in horror. "Who'd want to be like Uncle Tompkins?"

"Sometimes it's better that way," Drake said gravely.

"If you say so," I said uncertainly. It was a strange family who would want an Uncle Tompkins dragging around forever.

"What about this boy Tommy, Samantha?" asked Lupi. "Is he dead or alive?"

"What a question!" I laughed. "He's alive, of course. And probably wishes I were dead."

"Is he frightening?" she asked.

"I don't know him that well," I replied. What do you say to a question like that? He was frightening because at one time I felt something for him and I didn't know how he felt about me. But I didn't care anymore. Now, he could get lost as far as I was concerned.

"I think it's exciting to fall in love with someone who frightens you," said Lupi.

"Lupi, I didn't know you were such a romantic," I said.

She smiled.

"Do you like the Blob?" I asked.

Drake giggled.

"No." Lupi hardly considered it. "I don't think the Blob is very romantic at all. It's scary, but it isn't a loving monster. I like loving monsters."

"I wonder how many loving monsters there are in the world," I speculated.

"My father says there aren't enough," Drake said very seriously. "That's why he formed the Monster Preservation Society for Endangered Species."

"No kidding?" I really didn't believe this, but like most of their other stories, I figured I'd better go along with it.

"Yes. They've done some very important work in encouraging monsters to stick together," Drake explained.

"Our father is a hero," Lupi added. "Did you notice?"

"Well, er, there is definitely something different about him," I said, smiling. There was something downright odd about him, but I didn't say so. Maybe the Monster Preservation Society held all those conferences that they attended. I never even knew such a group existed in Plainview.

We went back to watching Godzilla versus King Kong, but I had trouble concentrating. I kept wondering, was there really a Monster Preservation Society in town? I could ask Iris—maybe she had heard of them—but I wasn't sure I wanted to know.

When the movie ended, Drake flipped on the lights. "May I have some of those krispies?" I asked him.

"Sure, have some," he said, offering me the bag.

I glanced inside this time and recoiled in horror.

"Samantha, what's wrong?" Lupi cried.

I stared inside the bag. I should have known.

"What's wrong with them?" she insisted.

Have you ever tasted something without seeing it, and imagined what it looked like just from the taste? Well, that was what had happened to me. I had imagined the krispies to be like potato chips: the sour-cream-and-onion kind. But they looked altogether different. They were green and all crinkled.

"What did you say these were called?" I asked.

"Dragon Krispies," said Drake.

As I said before, I should have known.

Chapter

11

After the Browns got their VCR, all the kids wanted to do was watch movies, which was okay by me. When I went over on Friday night, Lupi was watching *I Was a Teenage Werewolf.*

"Is it scary?" I asked.

"No. I don't think it's supposed to be," she replied simply.

I sat down next to her.

"I wanted to watch it to get ready for the full moon," she said, brushing her hair away from her face. She looked a little pale to me.

"Really? I didn't know there was a full moon tonight," I said.

"Look out the window."

I went to the window and saw the pale white globe of the moon in the darkening sky.

I grinned. "How do you get ready for a full moon?"

She shrugged. "Just be prepared."

"You always hear those stories about people going crazy during a full moon," I said, laughing. "Whenever I do a lot of strange things, my mother always says it must be due to the full moon."

Lupi looked at me with interest. Her eyes seemed a little yellow. "Really? I never heard that before. My mother never told me that."

"I thought everybody's mother told them that," I said.

Drake appeared in the doorway with a test tube full of something red and bubbling. "I have made a discovery," he announced.

"What is it?" I asked eagerly.

"Ketchup is made of tomatoes," he said simply. "Which means we can use it to make potions."

"Magic potions?" I asked.

"Yes." He held the test tube up to the light. The red liquid looked as clear as colored cellophane. "Look how pretty it is! I can make something extra special with this."

"Do you do that a lot—think up potions?" I asked.

"In my spare time," he told me. Then he wandered off, chanting to his ketchup.

I went back to watching the movie. Lupi pointed to the boy on the screen who was eventually going to turn into a werewolf.

"Now he's the cutest one in the movie, don't you think so?"

"He's pretty cute," I agreed.

"But he gets better, watch and see." A few minutes later, he turned into a werewolf, and started biting people to shreds. Pieces of torn and bloody clothing were left lying around all over the woods—the crime of the century.

Then they showed a shot of the werewolf with shreds of fabric hanging from his mouth and blood on his fur.

"There he is! Isn't he gorgeous?" Lupi cried excitedly.

"I think I liked him better the other way," I ventured.

But Lupi kept raving about him, and I noticed her voice changing. She cleared her throat.

"Lupi, do you have a cold or something?"

"Oh, no. I'm excited," she said, smiling at me. Her eyes had turned yellow and her mouth looked funny.

"Your eyes look yellow in this light. I thought they were blue," I noted.

"Sometimes blue and sometimes yellow," she explained. Then she went up to the screen and kissed it. "I just love this movie!"

"He's in a werewolf costume, Lupi, he's not real," Drake reminded her as he sat down in one of those swallowing chairs.

I went out of the room to get some juice and

cookies which I'd brought for the movie watching. When I came back into the room, Lupi was jumping around on all fours.

I laughed. "What're you trying to be? A monkey?" Seeing Lupi on the ground like that, I suddenly had the bright idea to introduce the kids to the game of charades. I quickly explained the rules to them.

"Great! We can do our favorite movies," suggested Lupi.

Drake went first. He oozed along the ground, grabbing at our legs.

"I know!" cried Lupi. "He's the Blob!"

I went next. Who was my favorite movie character? I imitated the lead singer from a popular rock movie.

Lupi jumped up and clapped her hands. "I know who you are! I've seen her on MTV—it's Raunchy Rhonda and the Rondelles!" she crowed.

"Hey, Lupi, that's it! You watch MTV?" I asked.

"Yeah, it's my favorite," she replied, still in that raspy voice.

Then it was Lupi's turn. After getting down on all fours again, she bounded around the room. Her eyes glittered and she growled deep in her throat.

"We're not supposed to use sound effects, Lupi," I reminded her.

I noticed she had animal hair all over her

hands. "You're wearing gloves, too," I said. "I don't know whether those are allowed."

"I don't think those are gloves, Samantha," Drake corrected me.

"How could they be anything else? She doesn't have hairy hands, does she?" I said, jokingly.

"Only sometimes," answered Drake.

"Okay, Lupi, we've already guessed who you are," I said. "You're the werewolf in *I Was a Teenage Werewolf.*"

When she wagged her head, I noticed how shaggy she'd become. Her hair was all bushy and her face seemed really grotesque and kind of bumpy. What was that: hair . . . on her face?

"Lupi, what's wrong with you?" I cried. Then I saw that her clothes looked funny. Her pink Spiderman T-shirt had stretched out to the limit, and she had hair running up and down her arms—not the normal amount of hair that comes with arms, but thick animal-like hair.

All of a sudden, Lupi didn't look like herself anymore. I wondered, had I missed something? But I didn't have time to think, because instantly, she lunged at me.

I screamed. Something sharp ripped my shirt sleeve. Backing away from her, I stumbled over one of the swallowing chairs. She was all hair.

"You-you're a werewolf! You're not really. You *can't* be," I stammered, and then I just screamed—and screamed! I tore through the house, screaming. The bat fluttered down from the rafters and flew frantically around the room as Drake and Lupi ran after me.

"Samantha!" Lupi cried. "Don't be scared. It's just me. I'm sorry. I was only kidding."

Finally, I stopped running and turned around, but she was still a werewolf. Drake came over to stand by my side.

"You're *kidding?* How can you be kidding? Are you real?" I demanded.

"I'm really a werewolf," she answered, "but I was only kidding about attacking you. It was just for fun. I won't hurt you. Honest."

As I looked into those yellow animal eyes, I wondered how in the world I could trust a monster.

"Why didn't you just tell me you were a werewolf?" I asked. "Why did you let me think you were normal?"

"I guess I just forgot about it," she said. "And a lot of people get upset about werewolves, because when they make movies about them, they put them in such a bad light."

"That's true. I would never make friends with one," I replied—but then I quickly realized what I'd just said. "I mean, I guess I wouldn't have made friends with you so easily if I'd known you as a werewolf first."

"I understand," said Lupi.

"I've seen you look like that before, but I always thought you were wearing a costume. I mean, when do you turn into one? Only during a full moon?"

Drake started laughing at me. "That's only in the movies, Samantha. Lupi can become a werewolf almost any time." But he suddenly stopped laughing and looked at me gravely. "There is one thing about the full moon, though: that's when she gets really dangerous."

"D-Dangerous?" I stuttered. A chill ran all the way from the roots of my hair down to my toes.

"I usually stay inside when there's a full moon—locked up," Lupi said. "You might as well know that. It's part of the babysitting job."

"Right." I shuddered.

"By the way, Samantha, sorry about my claws," she said. "Sometimes I don't know my own strength."

I glanced down at my ripped shirt sleeve, which hung from my shoulder in tattered ribbons. I shuddered again. "Claws? You did this with your *claws?*"

"Sure." With that, Lupi proudly displayed her three-inch claws.

"How did you get to be a werewolf, Lupi?

94

Does it run in the family or something?" I asked.

"My father is part werewolf," she said seriously.

Closing my eyes, I collapsed against the wall. "Somebody please tell me I'm dreaming," I groaned, before passing out.

When I woke up, everything was a little out of focus. Drake knelt beside me, looking concerned, and Lupi stood over us. She offered to get me a glass of water, but she still looked like a werewolf.

"Are you okay, Samantha?" she asked.

"No," I said bluntly. I'd just been through an ordeal. A girl turning into a werewolf? No, it couldn't happen. Impossible.

Chapter
═══12═══

On Saturday, I told Iris about Lupi.

"There's no such thing as a werewolf, Samantha," Iris stated flatly—which made me regret that I'd told her, but I had to tell someone!

How can you walk around with that kind of knowledge burning a hole in you? You have to tell someone eventually, and since Iris was my best friend, I had to choose her.

In such a normal setting, sitting in Iris' bedroom eating corn chips and drinking soda, I wanted to believe her. I wanted to believe there was no such thing as a werewolf.

"Iris, I know what I saw, and I saw a werewolf over there. It wasn't anybody dressed up in a costume," I insisted.

"Lupi only *acted* like a werewolf, she can't *be* one," Iris said.

"Maybe it seems that way to you, but I know what I saw."

"Look, Sam." Iris patted me on the back. "There's a full moon, and it's almost Halloween. People get a little crazy at this time of year. And with all this stuff we've been doing for the Halloween party, it's probably just gone to your head."

"Yeah, right. Just call me Slimehead," I said. I was kind of mad that she refused to take me seriously. "You've always believed me before, and I've always believed you, Iris. So I'm going to tell you what else has happened over there."

"Yeah, go ahead," Iris said. "That's what friends are for."

"I already told you about their Uncle Tompkins who smells like you wouldn't believe. And they have the most disgusting food, Iris, like nothing you've ever seen before."

"Yeah, you told me. Maybe they're gourmets or something," she suggested.

"No, they like black, burned food and weird things. It's not trendy—it's freaky food."

"Maybe you need to think about something else, Sam. How about Halloween decorations? You're really flipping out, you know that?" Sighing deeply, Iris looked at me as though I'd gone completely bonkers.

Well, maybe she was right. I was beginning to wonder, too.

* * *

For the next few days, we spent most of our time getting ready for the party. I tried not to think about the Browns at all, but I kept breaking out in a cold sweat. I had gotten clumsy, like Harry the handyman ghost. Here we were, creating a haunted house, and I was the one that felt haunted.

On Thursday, the night before the Halloween party, I brought the decorations over to the Browns' house to put the finishing touches on them. I still had a little sewing and gluing left to do. Plus, I wanted to see what the Browns thought of Slime and Creepy Crawlies.

Kimmie was visiting, and of course she was very curious about everything. She watched me open the bag of Creepy Crawlies and right away her pudgy hand scooped one up. "Mine!" she cried with delight.

"Oh, okay, Kimmie, you can have that one," I said generously, thinking that it would keep her out of mischief.

"What is this substance?" Drake asked, fingering the Slime.

"I don't know what it's made of, but it's so gross that it'll be great for a haunted house," I said.

"I'd like to experiment with it," he told me, "if you have any extra."

"I'll give you some after the party, okay?" I

promised. Slime cost a lot of money, and we had only enough for the haunted house.

"I think you should put it in the skulls," Lupi suggested. "You can borrow our skulls."

"But your decorations . . ." I protested.

She fluttered her hand casually. "Don't worry, Samantha. We have extras." With that, she thrust a small skull into my hands, while Drake wandered into his laboratory. Briefly, I wondered which relative I was holding.

Drake came out of the lab holding a beaker of clear yellow liquid. "I created this for one of our relatives, Aunt Sweena."

I admired the liquid, figuring that it must have some special properties. "I'm sure your aunt will just love it, Drake," I said.

I sat down and began sewing plastic spiders onto the big spiderweb. As he peered into the bag of Creepy Crawlies, Drake slowly dribbled some of his Aunt Sweena's yellow liquid onto them, then onto the container of Slime with Eyeballs.

"What are you doing?" I cried, jumping up and stabbing myself with the needle as I did so.

He smiled. "Oh, Samantha, don't worry. I just thought I could make them better with a little of this. It's pretty valuable stuff, you know."

"I'm sure it is, but I don't want any of

it . . ." His face clouded, and I immediately felt bad for hurting his feelings. I added quickly, "I mean, I don't want them to change color or shrivel up or anything like that," I babbled nervously.

"Sure, but this won't hurt them, honest," he said sweetly. He was such a sweet kid.

"Okay, I believe you," I replied, but I was trembling.

Lupi came over and patted my hand comfortingly. "Drake, I think Samantha is upset. I've got an idea. Samantha, why don't we all go and help you with the haunted house? We could be very helpful."

I shuddered. "Oh, I'm sure you could be, Lupi. It's very nice of you to offer. But I'll have to work at the haunted house, so I wouldn't be able to watch you guys."

"Maybe our parents can bring us to the party," Drake suggested. I guess he had read the look on my face when I answered Lupi. I was afraid to bring her if she might get "dangerous." "Don't worry, Samantha," Drake assured me, "I'll keep an eye on Lupi."

"I'll be good, Samantha," Lupi insisted. "Let's all go to the party together."

"Let's do that. Mother and Father would enjoy it, too," Drake said.

When Dr. and Mr. Brown arrived home, they told me that although they didn't want to go to the party themselves, they would be happy to drop the children off.

I breathed uneasily. I knew the kids would have fun there, but I wasn't so sure I wanted to be responsible for them in my school—especially after the store incident—even if Drake *could* take care of Lupi. You just never knew what they were going to think of, do—or turn into—next.

Chapter

===13===

On Friday night, Iris and I left my house, armed with the skull, dummies, Creepy Crawlies, cold spaghetti, the battery-operated moving hand, Slime with Eyeballs, and a few other ghastly odds and ends.

"Have we got everything?" Iris asked.

"I think so. I can't think of anything else. Oh, I asked the janitor if we could use the vacuum cleaner, so it's all set," I told her. Of course, the janitor had thought I was crazy. No kid at school asks to use the vacuum cleaner unless forced to by a teacher, and I hadn't wanted to go into the whole story of how we planned to make the vacuum cleaner into a ghost.

My mother was waiting in the car, revving the engine impatiently. She studied Iris in her

Swiss cheese costume. "Is this a food festival or a Halloween party?" she asked.

"Oh, Mom," I groaned.

"I should've worn last year's costume," Iris said. She turned to me. "Remember last year's?"

"How could I forget?" Iris was a mad computer brain last year. She had raced around beeping at everybody. As for me, I wore my black leotard cat suit, as planned.

Just as we were getting out of the car, I dropped the bag of "decorations."

Mom laughed when she saw what we had brought to the party. "Looks like you're going to have a real house of horror," she said.

"That's just what we want," Iris told her. "The most horrible haunted house ever."

By this time the word "horrible" sort of turned me off. Nobody realized how deeply involved I was in horror—only Iris, and she didn't really believe me. She thought I was nuts. Things had definitely changed between us since I had confided in her about the Browns. I knew she was worried about hanging out with a complete lunatic. Who wouldn't be? Sometimes I worried about hanging out with myself. Let's face it, you are judged by the company you keep. So Iris kept giving me these fish-eyed looks, like any moment she expected me to turn into a monster or something.

Anyway, as I scooped up the Creepy Crawlies, the container of cold pasta fell onto the street. Dropping things was becoming a habit with me.

"Oh, Samantha! You are clumsy lately," my mother sighed, and I knew she was remembering that I'd dropped a dozen cupcakes on their frosted heads a few days earlier.

"Nobody's perfect," I muttered, gathering up my stuff.

We went straight to the auditorium. Iris had found some shiny black curtains at a rummage sale, and we hung them at the front entrance, which was really the side door of the stage.

Then I turned off the lights. "Hey, look. Did you know the eyeballs glow in the dark?" I yelled to Iris.

She climbed down from the stepladder to take a look. "Yuck. They're gross," she said.

"Good. Now let's have the worms."

Iris dumped the spaghetti into a bowl. "Someone will have to shove people's hands into this," she reminded me.

We stuck rubber spiders and Creepy Crawlies on the inside of the curtains and dangled some from the rafters so they would brush against the tops of people's heads.

"A lot of little kids will come, so let's put them at kid level," I suggested.

"But the bigger people like us will get

Creepy Crawlies in our mouths and up our noses," objected Iris.

"You can't have everything."

Iris went to get the skeleton from the science teacher's room. I set up the battery-operated moving hand on a music stand, so that it looked like it would grab at people. We decided to hang up some monster masks and also rigged up some cheap plastic eyeglasses so that the Slime with Eyeballs peered through them.

Anyone who has ever played with Slime could never forget the experience. It sticks to you like glue, it's green, and it has the appearance of something that I'm not even going to mention here. But with the glasses and in the masks, it created a fantastic effect. I started to get excited. I wished Lupi and Drake were here. I was glad their parents would be bringing them later, because they would certainly be impressed.

Mr. Roach, the janitor, brought the upright vacuum cleaner. "Never could figure out why kids would want a vacuum," he grumbled. "What are you using it for?"

"A ghost." Iris launched into her demonstration. She grabbed her prepared sheet and threw it over the machine, immediately transforming it into a ghost. "Watch this." She plugged it in and—varoom!—the "ghost" roared, its wrappings fluttering menacingly.

"Hey, I like that. Pretty nifty," Mr. Roach said admiringly.

After Mr. Roach had rattled off his instructions on where to leave the vacuum when we were done, Iris asked me, "Don't you like it, Sam?"

"Yes, very authentic."

Just then, a bumblebee and a can of soda walked in.

"Hi, guys. What's left to do?" the bumblebee asked.

I quickly identified them as Allison Rumby and Shannon Blackwell, two girls who had reluctantly agreed to help us with the haunted house. Of course, we hadn't seen them since we started the committee, but I suppose their appearance was better late than never.

"It's about time you showed up," Iris said in her huffiest tone.

"We'll leave if you want us to," replied Allison, putting her hands on her ample bumblebee hips.

I jabbed Iris in the ribs. I didn't want her overreacting. After all, we *could* use their help. "Come on. Don't *bug* them," I said, making Iris burst out laughing. Then I turned to Shannon and Allison. "We're glad you're here, aren't we, Iris? We need all the help we can get."

That statement was going to prove truer than we realized at the time. The girls were waiting for something to do, so I turned into an instant organizer. "Now, we need the skeleton in the corner over here, and we have this black light to shine on it. I'll leave that up to you. When you're finished, come back and I'll find something else for you to do."

Shannon stared at the skeleton. "Was it a boy or a girl?"

"I don't know, Shannon. You'll have to ask Mr. Rendt. It's his skeleton," I said, turning my attention back to the Slime with Eyeballs.

Then Allison started moaning about how her bumblebee costume made it impossible to work.

"Hey, Allison, haven't you ever heard the expression, 'busy as a bee'?" I asked.

She gave me a withering glance, looking incredibly stuffy in her bumblebee suit. If a real bee looked at you that way, you'd cringe.

I concentrated on getting the Slime with Eyeballs set up just right, so a person would have the image of going into a room with all the eyes on him or her. I stuck some of them on the inside of the curtain, and I put some others inside the monster masks and in the skull. Then I turned on an electric fan at low speed, which made all the hanging things move just a little bit. Iris propped most of the dummies in corners, but she left a few lying on the floor for people to trip over.

Finally we were ready. Allison and Shannon

conveniently got lost. I asked Maurice Maklo-
witz, who has a crush on me, to dunk people's
hands in the spaghetti worms, and as payment,
he could go through the haunted house for
free. Iris borrowed a big roll of tickets from the
attendance office, and we set up a card table
outside the stage door with a box to collect all
the money. I put Patrick's spooky tape on the
cassette player. Before long kids started to
trickle in, and I noticed Tommy Deere standing a little apart from the other boys, as he
often does. I quickly had to remind myself
that I was still mad at him. I closed my eyes,
wishing that he would come over and buy a
ticket from me.

"Sam, open your eyes," ordered Iris. "You
look like you're in a trance, and here comes
Tommy Deere, headed straight for us."

I immediately felt my cheeks grow hot and I
let out a dumb sound as though I were in pain.

Tommy walked right up to me and looked
straight into my eyes. (I know that sounds
corny, but it's true.) I stared back at him,
trying hard to hold onto the fact that I had
been mortally embarrassed because of him.
He had to be awful to let that happen. "Hi,
Sam. I'd like one ticket, please," he said.

"Sure," I said, grateful for the opportunity
to look down at the fat roll of tickets. I tore off
a ticket—a simple enough task, but I handed it

to him as though it were a check for a hundred dollars.

"Thanks." He shifted from one foot to the other. He looked around to make sure that his friends had lined up on Iris' side. I opened my mouth to say "next, please" in my most important voice, when he said, "Hey, uh, about the other day . . ."

"Yeah? When?" I asked nonchalantly, while my heart pounded.

"You know, the other day in my father's store." He turned beet red. "I'm sorry about what happened, that's all. It wasn't fair and I know it wasn't your fault."

"Oh, that!" I clapped my hand over my forehead in "sudden dawning understanding" —as though it had been so insignificant, I had never given it another thought. That's me, Samantha Slade, skimming through life. Sticks and stones may break my bones, but being kicked out of your father's store will never hurt me. "Oh, that's okay," I said. "I'm sorry, too."

He nodded, blushing still. "Yeah. Well, okay then. I just wanted to tell you."

I smiled, feeling satisfied. He apologized for being so mean! I was so excited.

"What was that all about?" Iris wanted to know.

I barely heard her. Randy Alsip stood in

front of me, buying a ticket. I couldn't talk about this exciting moment with all these people around.

"I'll tell you later," I said. As a few kids slipped inside the curtain, some great screams erupted. I could tell what they were looking at—first, the vacuum cleaner, the skull, then the spaghetti, then the Slime with Eyeballs, the dummies lying on the floor, the hand trying to grab them, and the Creepy Crawlies grazing their heads.

When people emerged from the other side of the stage, they were all laughing and talking excitedly.

"Did you see that skeleton? I thought it was coming after me," a girl said.

"How did they get all those eyeballs in there like that?"

"And real worms! They had real worms!" another boy shrieked.

"Those weren't worms, that was just spaghetti," a girl scoffed.

"There are dead bodies in there," somebody yelled.

Suddenly, a blood-chilling scream ripped through the auditorium. Everyone gasped and turned toward the haunted house. Silence followed. I stared at Iris, as though I expected some sort of answer out of her, but she looked back at me blankly.

Three people ran toward us from the haunted house exit.

"Look, they're coming out the entrance, too!" cried Iris. She hurried over to them. "Hey, what's going on? You have to go through the whole haunted house. It's a one-way trip!"

"No way!" a fat little boy shot back. "I'm not going in there *ever* again! Those creatures are crawling all over the place." He shuddered visibly.

"Oh, don't worry," I whispered. "I put a fan on them. They only *look* like they're moving."

Iris frowned at me. "Why are you telling him one of your secrets? Let him be scared half to death, dummy."

Another scream tore through the air, but this one warbled and trailed out of the curtained house with a girl from my class, Tina Mateo. She pointed her shaking finger back at the house.

"They're coming this way!" she cried. "Run, everybody, run!"

Suddenly this whole thing looked and sounded like a scene from *The Blob*. The way these people were carrying on, any minute something was going to come oozing out of my haunted house. I jumped up.

"Now, wait a minute," I shouted. "There's nothing in there that I can't explain. Iris and I made everything and we know exactly . . ."

A bunch of screams that blended into one long howl cut my words off, as a group of students struggled to get through the small entranceway—backward. I felt like saying "No big deal, guys. Buy a ticket and join the fun," because I didn't think there was any real danger, and because I really thought that I'd done a great job of scaring people. I mean, I never knew . . .

Bug-eyed Phyllis Marshall came up to me. "The Creepy Crawlies are alive! Samantha, *do* something! They're alive!" she cried, her face pressed up so close to mine that I could smell her peppermint breath.

"Phyllis, calm down, please. As I was telling this boy over here, I purposely put a fan in there . . ."

"Samantha, do you *know* what's going on inside your haunted house?" Tommy had run up to me, white as a sheet. A girl stood behind him clutching her face in horror.

"Well, I think I should know, Tommy, because it was my idea and I know everything that I put in there." I tried to sound like an authority, because I was.

"I can't stand it. The eyes *blinked* at me," the horrified girl said.

"They can't blink!" I cried. "They're just Slime with Eyeballs. You buy them in a toy store. I bought them myself!"

"The Creepy Crawlies are coming!" Another student ran out of the exit, waving his arms around wildly. "They're all over the place! Help! Help!"

"Ahhhhhhhhhhhh!" A scream turned into a gurgle, and I saw its owner run past me.

"Samantha, LOOK BEHIND YOU!" Tommy yelled.

I whirled around, and then I saw THEM. The Creepy Crawlies were slithering down the curtains and along the wooden floors, leaving bright silvery trails behind them. They looked more disgusting than ever, as their squishy bodies advanced menacingly toward us. *But why were they moving?* I asked myself.

Next to me, Iris screamed her head off. I had this brief feeling that I should stay there, even though everyone else was running away from the haunted house as quickly as possible. I thought "the captain should not give up the ship," but then Iris shook my shoulder vigorously, no doubt trying to knock some sense into me. It took me a couple of seconds, and then I shouted, "RUN for it! They're really alive!"

Iris, Tommy, and I ran out of the auditorium toward the staircase, which was crowded with students trying to escape.

"Some mess you got us into this time, Samantha," huffed Iris.

"Now wait a minute, Iris. *I* didn't do this. How could I make a bunch of Creepy Crawlies come alive?"

"You could've bought something at the magic store," Iris accused me. I realized right then that she saw everything in completely black-and-white terms, and she liked it that way. That's why she believed I was responsible. There had to be a logical reason for everything with her—and that's why she couldn't believe me when I told her about the Browns.

Tommy looked at me questioningly.

"I didn't *do* anything," I insisted.

"Don't worry about it now." Impatiently, Tommy grabbed my hand and the three of us pressed through the crush of people, down a flight of stairs and out into the night.

As we were running, I remembered everything. Last night, Drake had poured his potion on my Creepy Crawlies and on the big container of Slime with Eyeballs. He had made the potion for a relative and thought it would make the Creepy Crawlies "better."

The only possible explanation was that the potion had activated the Creepy Crawlies and made them come alive! Although I had noticed that the Browns liked dead things, like plants, they seemed to want to keep their relatives and friends "around" in any form. The living dead were normal and welcome in that household—

like Uncle Tompkins, for instance, or their shrunken heads. I wondered how many members of their family had been given a second life in the Browns' laboratory. Probably Drake's Aunt Sweena was dead, and he intended to bring her to life, too.

But I couldn't tell anyone that. No one would believe me. I saw Iris looking at me as though she didn't really know me, and I suddenly felt as if it *were* all my fault.

"I know it wasn't your fault," Tommy was saying, "but maybe someone did something to them while you weren't looking. Maybe they put motors on them. I read about an experiment like that in *Popular Science* once, where someone put little motors on stuffed animals."

"Oh, yeah?" I brightened at the idea.

"Yeah, it's the only logical explanation."

"Gee, I'm glad you thought of that," I breathed, wondering what the school principal would think of that explanation. "But what if we don't find little motors on the Creepy Crawlies?"

Tommy shrugged. "Gee, I don't know, Samantha. I guess we think of something else."

The schoolground looked as though everyone had come out for a fire drill, except that it wasn't orderly and there were no teachers standing around telling everyone to be quiet.

Mr. Owens, the principal, marched directly toward us.

"Uh-oh, here comes trouble," muttered Tommy, straightening to attention.

"Hi, Mr. Owens," I said sweetly.

"Samantha and Iris, I'd like to have a word with you privately in my office," he said.

Naturally, we agreed. This was no time to argue.

Iris turned a poisonous look toward me. As we followed Mr. Owens, I tried to think of something to say to fix the situation, but there wasn't anything I could say. The bottom line was: we were in big trouble. Even worse: we were doomed.

Chapter
=14=

"Fortunately, the Creepy Crawlies have been arrested," Mr. Owens said as we followed him back inside the building.

"Arrested?" Iris and I chorused. Both of us were thinking the same thing—whoever heard of a Creepy Crawlie being arrested?

"Well, they are no longer moving. Whatever caused them to move has stopped motivating them."

"That's good," I said. We had reached the office. I thought briefly about how I had intended to run for class president, but I guessed I could forget that plan.

Mr. Owens sat at his desk and pressed his fingertips together to form a steeple. "We don't want this story to get around. It's rather unbelievable, but I'm sure you have a logical explanation, which I trust you will tell me now."

"I don't know anything," Iris insisted.

I glared at her. Thanks, Iris. "Mr. Owens, we didn't know the Creepy Crawlies were going to move," I said in a rush. "I turned the fan on them so they would move just a little bit, but there's no way to make them ... walk around," I gulped.

"Yes, well, that's what I thought. The idea of them moving is impossible, isn't it?" Mr. Owens gazed into my eyes. Actually, he stared at me until I squirmed uncomfortably. "So that even though we both know this to be impossible, it has happened," he said softly.

Iris shifted in her seat.

"It's not our fault," I said. "And Iris didn't even *buy* the Creepy Crawlies, so she is even less at fault."

"Samantha, I admire you for wanting to protect your friend, but we must get to the bottom of this. The children will leave school tonight scared out of their wits—due entirely to your irresponsible action."

I started to get mad, because I was not irresponsible, and I thought he was a jerk for saying so. But just then two shadows passed across the floor.

"Excuse me," a familiar voice said. I turned around. Drake and Lupi, looking like her werewolf self, stood in the doorway. I cringed, thinking it was all over for me. What if she became dangerous? "I know Samantha, and she is *not* irresponsible."

"That's true, Mr. Owens," I said, quickly jumping to my own defense. "I'm not irresponsible at all. Just ask anyone."

"Oh?" said Mr. Owens, looking a little surprised. His glasses slipped down his long nose.

A group of kids had gathered outside Mr. Owens' office to look at Lupi.

"Wow, what a great costume," they were saying.

"You look like a real werewolf," one kid told her. "Who did your make-up?"

Lupi smiled. "It's real."

"Hey! Let's go back to that haunted house. It's great!" someone yelled.

"Really?" Mr. Owens sounded surprised. "But I thought it was too frightening."

"Not anymore. Look." Drake pointed in the direction of the haunted house. Kids were lining up to go through it again.

This was my chance to take a real stand. After all, I had nothing to lose.

"Mr. Owens, Iris and I formed a committee to come up with a *real* haunted house, one that people would talk about for a long time," I began. "It was *supposed* to be scary."

"It's a great house," said Lupi. "It's just like home."

Mr. Owens laughed. "I hardly think you

can compare this haunted house with your home."

Little did he know. Lupi stood in front of Mr. Owens, her eyes turning yellow-green, just like they did when she turned into a werewolf. For one terrible moment, I thought she might hurt him. Instead, she just smiled her charming werewolf smile.

Mr. Owens smiled back. Then he looked over our heads at the crowd gathering at the entrance to the haunted house.

"See?" I persisted. "Everyone loves the haunted house. They love being scared. That's what we wanted. And besides, it's really good for the school. I think it will raise a lot of money."

He raised his eyebrows when I said "money." I guess he was a little like me in that way. "You've caused a lot of trouble to this student body, Samantha," he said, "but it looks like your party is a huge success."

"You're right. The kids love it, Mr. Owens," agreed Iris, but he didn't seem to hear.

"Everyone's having a great time," Lupi said.

"Well, okay then." Mr. Owens smiled. "Let's join the party."

We followed Mr. Owens into the auditorium.

"I thought we were dead," Iris whispered. "I think what you said made him change his mind."

"Maybe. But he also saw how successful we were," I replied. "And I'm sure he's thinking about how much money we'll make for the school. He knows how hard it is to raise money, so maybe he'll actually thank us one of these days."

"I think the best comes out in people at Halloween," said Lupi.

Iris and I gave her puzzled looks, but she didn't seem to notice. We had arrived on the scene.

Mr. Owens even put on one of the monster masks we had brought to the gym with us!

Tommy and a bunch of the other kids were picking up Creepy Crawlies and placing them back in the haunted house. I felt grateful to him for restoring order to the mess.

"I'm glad to see you kids doing such a good job." Mr. Owens patted Tommy on the shoulder.

Tommy looked at Mr. Owens and then at me, completely surprised by the change in the principal.

"I think the haunted house will make a lot of money for the school," said Mr. Owens. "Just look at all those happy kids!"

Iris took her place at the ticket table, and Drake and Lupi lined up along with everyone else.

"Oh, you don't have to pay," I told them. "How can I ever thank you for showing up when you did? If it weren't for you . . ." I began.

Lupi held up her hand. "No, Samantha, we owed you one, remember?"

She and her brother smiled. We were all remembering the incident at Tommy's father's store.

"By the way, Samantha, my mom spoke to Mr. Deere about the store, and she said she'll take care of everything," Drake explained. "It wasn't your fault, and our mom and dad will pay for the damages."

"Wow, thanks!" I exclaimed. I had been really worried about owing all that money— especially for something I didn't do.

Mr. Owens went through the haunted house himself and came out saying it was a wonderful experience. Later, when the auditorium had filled with people, he made an announcement.

"Ladies and gentlemen! Now that most of you have had a chance to go through our great haunted house, it's time for our Halloween contest for the most original costume! Will those who wish to enter please line up on the stage here next to me?"

"Why don't you enter, Lupi?" I suggested. I was feeling a little more sure of her: she had remained pretty quiet since she'd been here, and she didn't seem too dangerous.

"But this isn't a costume, Samantha," she whispered. "It wouldn't be fair."

"Oh, that's right," I replied. "But how would anyone know?"

She smiled mysteriously before joining the others on the stage.

Iris entered the contest, too. She was not only the best slice of Swiss cheese there, but she was also the *only* slice of Swiss or any other kind of cheese. One boy had dressed up as a sneaker, with different colored novelty shoelaces tied together to make one big one. His face stuck out of the toe. Of course, the usual assortment of witches, ghosts, goblins, and space creatures—one of which was my bratty brother, Patrick—had showed up, too. Patrick wore styrofoam antennas sticking up from a headband, and a gross-looking mask with one eyeball hanging down over a disgusting mouth.

Suddenly Patrick left the stage and walked over to me. "Hey, Sam, that's a pretty neat haunted house. How did you do all that stuff?"

"Just brilliant, kid," I said, grinning at him.

"You used my scary record," he said, looking pleased.

"Yeah, thanks. It sounds great, doesn't it?" I looked at him, thinking he wasn't half bad. There are a few times like that when I look at my brother and we get along okay, but pretty soon that niceness between us disappears, and I'm ready to disown him again.

Mr. Owens called for everyone's attention. "We will now announce the winners of our contest. Third prize goes to Lupi Brown."

"Wow, who's she?" cried Patrick. "She looks so *real.*"

"She's one of the kids I babysit for," I told him.

"Really?" His eyes shone.

"Second prize to Wally Blake, the sneaker. And first prize goes to Iris Martin, the one and only slice of Swiss cheese!" Mr. Owens began clapping enthusiastically and everyone else joined in.

Iris was in her glory as she stepped up to receive her trophy. Then Lupi suddenly returned her prize ribbon to Mr. Owens and walked offstage. She walked down to where Drake was waiting and then over to me.

"We're leaving now, Samantha," she said. "It was a great party, thanks. But I can't take the prize. How can I win a prize just for looking the way I look?"

I almost mentioned that people enter beauty contests all the time just because they look the way they look, but I knew she wouldn't understand.

"Who *is* that girl?" someone asked, and a murmur traveled through the crowd as everybody tried to figure out who Lupi was and why she had given up the prize ribbon.

Patrick and I said goodbye to Lupi and Drake. I secretly thought that in spite of everything, it was fun being friends with a werewolf.

Chapter
══════15══════

The next day was Saturday—Halloween!—and Iris and I took the Browns out for trick-or-treat.

"I can't believe these kids," Iris declared, staring after Lupi, Drake, and Kimmie. "They're so weird. I mean, who has never seen a chocolate bar before?"

"I *told* you, Iris. They're very different," I said. It seemed like I'd been trying to convince her of this forever. I knew she wouldn't ever believe what was *really* different about the Browns, so I had pretty much given up trying.

Kimmie had dressed as a little devil, with real animal horns on her head and a fur costume with a peacock-feather tail. It wasn't my idea of a devil costume, but Lupi had put it together for her. Lupi had come up with this idea after checking out all the costumes at the Halloween party.

Drake had dressed in slacks and a shirt, with a bright red bow tie for the occasion.

Kimmie bounded up to the door of the next house, and squeaked, "Trick or treat!"

I followed closely behind, just in time to see a dish of candy float straight into her bag. As usual, Iris missed seeing this because she was joking around with some kids who were throwing eggs.

"Hey, young lady, don't you think you're being a little greedy?" the woman at the door asked.

"Greedy?" Kimmie blinked at her in surprise.

"Kimmie, put some of the candy back, please," I ordered, but she still stood there looking dumbfounded. Finally, I scooped the candy back into the dish. "Sorry about that," I said to the lady.

"You should teach her some manners," the lady replied scornfully.

"What was that all about?" Iris asked, running to catch up to us.

"Oh, nothing," I answered mildly, not wanting to tell Iris what had just happened. She would just tell me I was crazy, anyway.

"Boy, this is fun," she said, peering into

Lupi's trick-or-treat bag. "Do you know what this is?" she asked Lupi, holding up a bag of candy corn.

Lupi blinked at her. "No, but it's very colorful."

Iris laughed. Even though the kids had a-roused her curiosity, I think she thought Lupi and Drake were just kidding about the candy. I understood how she felt. Not so long ago, I had thought they were kidding, too.

HALLOWEEN PARTY
SCARING UP SUCCESS

The big Halloween party at Davis Junior High, sponsored by the seventh-grade class, was a huge success. Samantha Slade and Iris Martin created the scariest haunted house on record, which also got a record attendance!

The big hit of the haunted house was when the Creepy Crawlies were reported to have actually crawled. Those who saw them say it was horrible. But nobody has any proof. Did it happen or not?

Only Samantha Slade knows the answer to that question.

"Hey, Samantha," someone called to me from down the hall. I looked up from *The Davis Leader,* our school paper, to see who was calling. A bunch of people turned around to look at him. It was Tommy.

He walked over to me, smiling. "The party

was great," he said. He looked at the paper. "Did you read my article?"

"Yeah, thanks," I replied.

"Samantha, what do you really think happened with the Creepy Crawlies?" he asked me.

I just shrugged and smiled, feeling warm all over. I wasn't going to try to tell another person about my experience with the Browns. "That's confidential," I replied mysteriously.

I figured I was doing Tommy a big favor by keeping it a secret.

You'll never believe what happened later that fall . . .

It was hard enough for me to run for president of the seventh grade, but when Lupi and Drake started "helping" me, I was *really* doomed!

I mean, Iris (my campaign manager) and I were having a tough time in the first place running against Monica Hammond, who's only the most popular girl in the whole school. But then I made the mistake of tasting one of the formulas Drake had cooked up in his laboratory—something he called his "formula for greatness."

Well, I didn't think it was so great when I started turning into a *frog* in the middle of my campaign! Trying to dial a phone with my sticky webbed feet, staying away from the dissection table in the biology lab, making sure I didn't turn into my own cat's next meal . . . I'll tell you, it's not easy being a frog in the human world.

Don't worry, I'll tell you all about it later. Leap into action with SAMANTHA SLADE #2: *Confessions of a Teenage Frog,* available now.

About the Author

SUSAN SMITH was born in Great Britain and has lived most of her life in California. She began writing when she was thirteen years old and has authored a number of successful teenage novels, published in both hardcover and paperback. Currently, she lives in Brooklyn with her two children. Both children have provided her with many ideas and observations which she has included in her books. In addition to writing, Ms. Smith enjoys travel, horseback riding, skiing and swimming.